Mrs Saville

Also by Ted Morrissey

Mrs Saville

TED MORRISSEY

a novel

Twelve Winters Press

Published by Twelve Winters Press, a literary publisher.

P. O. Box 414 • Sherman, Illinois 62684-0414 • twelvewinters.com

Mrs Saville was first published by Twelve Winters Press in 2018. It is also available in hardcover and digital editions.

Cover and interior page design by the author.

Cover art copyright © 2018 Ted Morrissey.

Author photo copyright © 2018 Ted Morrissey.

ISBN
978-0-9987057-9-8

Printed in the United States of America

Acknowledgments

Early drafts of *Mrs Saville* were published serially at *Strands Lit Sphere* under various titles that do not appear in the final version. It is with sincere appreciation that I acknowledge Jose Varghese and his fellow editors at *Strands* and the *Lakeview Journal*. "A Wintering Place" first appeared in *Eleven Eleven*. Further thanks to Courtney Wick for her performance of an excerpt from *Mrs Saville* at the Hoogland Center for the Arts in Springfield, Illinois; the Louisville Conference on Literature and Culture Since 1900, University of Louisville, for an invitation to read from the novel in progress; and Pamm Collebrusco for her editing and unwavering support. Most of all, I wish to recognize Mary Wollstonecraft Shelley, whose life and masterpiece have been a never-ending source of inspiration for my own modest literary efforts.

for Melissa,
my Muse

Mrs Saville

On perceiving me, the stranger addressed me in English, although with a foreign accent. 'Before I come on board your vessel,' said he, 'will you have the kindness to inform me whither you are bound?'

— MARY W. SHELLEY, 'FRANKENSTEIN'

Dear Philip,

I have the most extraordinary news—Robin is home! He arrived quite unexpectedly, no advance word whatsoever, and I must say I did not at first recognise my own brother, he has changed so in these (can it be?) these *three years*. Agatha and I were with Mrs O'Hair in the kitchen boiling currants to put up (Mrs O is quite knowledgeable in the methods of preservation—the brutal Londonderry winters of her youth, she says—I know you will take to her and not find her *Irishness* unforgiveable), and I was slightly flustered because a bowl had slipped from Aggie's fingers and broken on the floor. I had just picked up the pieces and therefore did not hear Robin's conveyance stop before the house. Then Felix was in the kitchen reporting that a man was in the foyer. Heavens, I thought, Felix has let a beggar into the house—for who would be calling so early in the morning (the butcher's boy had already

been round to take our order); and Felix's sweet nature, well, you have said it, too much sugar can be a
deficiency. I was thinking perhaps I should send Felix to fetch Mr Smythe across the alley, to send away
the fellow—but I recalled Mr Smythe's gout has been
a particular bother of late, so I thought, no, I must see
to this new arrival. You have said that I must exercise
my will to run a proper home as lady of the house, my
dear, and I recalled it just then; so I dried my hands
and removed my apron, as not to offer the appearance
of a servant but rather said lady of the house, and went
to see to this stranger inside our door.

The moment I stepped from the kitchen, fragrant
with boiling currants, I was assailed by the streetbeg-
gar's odor, accented, I realised, with the tart smell of
the sea and its wretched wharfs—and perhaps it was
then that the idea of Robin's return began to come,
shyly, almost like a secret I was keeping from myself.
In the foyer, the first item I saw was his sailor's duffel
propped against the wall. It was a collage of unwholesome stains, and I half expected a gruesome yellow-in-
cisored rat to scurry from its ramshackle contents.

But my word, Philip—the fellow himself! *Frightful*
only barely begins to touch upon his appearance. His
topcoat was scarred with stitches and patches, its hem
come loose and frayed. His trousers were also stitched
and worn shiny and thin at the knee, his shoes a wreck,
one with the buckle absent altogether and made fast
by leather strings wove in an uneven web. I swear all
this came to me in the flash of a moment, as if I had

studied the poor wretch's portrait of an afternoon at the National.

But his face! Framed in a wild mane of hair, bleached seasalt grey, the same as his beard, both untouched by barber for months, if not years—it gave him the look of a lion, but not a powerful predator, rather an aged lion-emperor, his pride usurped, left to await the end, alone, and beaten.

Beneath the wild, untrimmed beard his cheeks were gaunt, which made me realise his overall thinness, like a refugee of famine. Even his fingers were elongated, the knuckles standing out like stones beneath the mummified skin, tarred black with dirt and dire circumstances. I thought at first the small and ring fingers of his left hand were oddly turned under, out of view, but no . . . they were missing—only their uneven stubs remained.

When I stepped toward him he turned his eyes upon me, and then I knew him, I knew my brother had returned after three years at sea. I knew him though I had never seen eyes like these: blue, yes, but the blue of ice, of seafrost, like his time in the Arctic waste had frostbitten his eyes, left them permanently cold and—I fear to write it, as if writing it may make it a sentence and a harbinger—cold and lifeless. They were as sterile as two silver coins, but coins which have been retrieved from the bottom of a well where their luster has been dulled over time.

'Poor Robin', I said—that was all I could say. I think I was in a state of shock. I had been wishing for my brother's safe return so ardently for so long . . . and here he was, alive—yes, but appearing to be a revenant, a phantom form of the man who sailed from Hastings that sunny day, captain of his own ship, which he christened the *Benjamin Franklin*, gallantly gleaming in the forecastle with fortitude and fearlessness.

Not a word for two whole years—the last letter had arrived from Arkhangelsk, more than six months in its own ragged travels. Excited still for the expedition, except a strain of loneliness had already crept into his pen and coloured the ink.

I am sorry, my darling, I am running on now about things you already know. It is just that I am lonely myself—I cannot speak with Mrs O'Hair, not as an equal of course, nor to the children. I do wish that you would conclude your affairs and return to us. That would set my spirits aright.

Sept 6—First, allow me to apologise for my self-indulgent lines above. I know you are toiling on our behalves, and I need not increase your burden by tossing on the weight of my loneliness. Who am I to claim loneliness in such a bustling house, under a roof and amid furnishings that your hard work has secured for us? My mind and my heart never forget it, my darling, but sometimes my hand runs ahead of my thoughts.

Please do not be upset, but I placed Robin in little Maurice's room—I knew not where else, and he does not have means for other lodging at the moment. Not to mention he needs looking after, the care of family, until he is quite himself again. I know that Robin's presence will be good for the children. They have missed a man in the house since you have been away. I do not mean to suggest that Robin can take your place, not for a moment do I mean it—but I must admit that even I anticipate feeling easier with him here. There have been many nights when I have felt your absence keenly and lay awake listening to every shift and shudder of this ancient house. And when the weather is warm, and the windows have to be raised, I am watchful indeed, starting at every noise from the street, every footfall, every voice, every shut door, every wincing hinge. Sometimes I rise from the empty-feeling bed and check on the children, at least that is what I tell myself, but in truth I think I am just seeking human companionship. At those dark hours I sense the weight of your long absence most acutely, and I just need to stand inside the children's doors and listen to their breathing. I do not bother with a candle for my vigil, not wanting to disturb them—and besides you have always said my powers to see in total gloom are positively feline. Though I fear all the stitchwork has dulled my eyes somewhat—but it fetches a few farthings, and I do enjoy it. I really do believe that had I the good fortune to have been born male I should have liked to have been a painter or some other sort of creative artist. Thank you for indulging my fantasies. I know you believe them unhealthy, and that it is better to stay grounded in the material world, where my nerves are steadier.

You are right to say, of course, and I do believe

my brother's return will help to cheer me. Between the clever husbandry of Mrs O'Hair and Robin's influence, I know I will be quite right again. Trust that I work against the sadness and bitterness I have felt since losing our little dove. Some days I feel I am conquering the emotions. And I do find writing to you a comfort. I hope my meandering missives are not too taxing upon you, for I would not wish to add to your cares—I know that the affairs which keep you away must be very tiring and troublesome indeed.

I have been away from the page, and now describe a later incident. There was a most terrible shouting— one would think a murder was being enacted—and at first I believed it was from the street. I was working at my stitching in the kitchen (in the morning the light is so much brighter there than in the parlour), and Mrs O and I looked upon each other quite startled, and I wondered at Felix, whether he was out of doors— but then the shouting continued and I realised it was coming from *inside* the house. I went to the hall, where both Felix and Agatha were standing holding hands, for the children too were a little shocked, and I realised the voice must be coming from Maurice's room, that it was Robin who was crying out. Mrs O had followed me to the hall, and I asked her to take the children to the kitchen for some milk while I saw to my brother. I went upstairs and tapped on Maurice's door; I did not anticipate a lucid reply as I could hear Robin speaking, though in no coherent manner. I gently opened the door. The curtains were shut tight, which rendered the room most gloomy, yet I saw well enough to notice that Robin had ejected the blankets from himself and they lay upon the floor, twisted and tangled. Robin was on the bed in a spasmodic reclination, and even with the dim lighting I could see that he had perspired through his nightshirt and beads were still heavy upon his brow. I quickly turned away when I comprehended Robin's state of undress. I thought for a moment that my entering the room had stirred him and he was speaking to me, except his words carried no meaning. I used my hand to shield his nakedness from my sight and I looked at his face, his eyes darting to and fro beneath their lids, and his lips muttering the inarticulate sounds. I listened closely to try to snatch a word or two, but I was not even certain then that he spoke English in his day-terror. Robin was always a quick student of languages, and who knows in his long travels what strange tongues he has acquired. That thought made me recall Acts: What if Robin is a messenger of some sort? And I recalled my doubting of Him—I had prayed so fervently at little Maurice's bedside, begging God to heal Maurice's lungs. You tried to pull me away, my darling, urging me to rest myself, reminding me that Agatha and Felix needed their mother. But I knew if I was devoted enough, if I pulled the pleas to spare our little dove from my very soul, spaded them up from my blackest, richest soil, soaked in my very heart's blood—God would hear them and would be moved to act.

But no. Instead I had to hold Maurice's hand while

he slowly drowned in his own bed. I often dream of the small hand that went from feverishly hot to cadaverously cold in my desperate grip.

What if this is the prayer that God answered? He has returned my brother to me, as if resurrected from the dead, for that is how I had begun to think of him, dead and gone, his body sarcophagused in ice. Now he is returned and perhaps bearing a message. It would be a comfort to believe in Him again, to feel His presence and not an utter void in the dark night—

Listen to me! Or rather do not! You will think I have gone daft. Spinning on about such stuff better left to philosophers of divinity.

Robin seemed to settle himself and was calmer in his sleep, so I crept from the room and went to reassure the children, who, I discovered, were quite content under Mrs O's gentle hand. She had given them some sweetbread soaked in milk—just a small wedge; she is mindful not to spoil their appetites. Mrs O developed an attachment to the children promptly when she came. There is something in her eyes when she looks upon them, Felix especially, that seems to be recognition, as if they remind her of other children, her own perhaps—but the memories would have to be very old ones as she is well beyond her childbearing years, well into her fifties I should think, maybe even sixty. The word that comes to mind when I think of Mrs O is *grey*—grey hair, yes, and eyes, and her two everyday frocks are shades of grey too. Yet it is more than all that: There is a grey cast that forms a sort of

backdrop in spite of her generally cheerful and industrious demeanor. It is like she has emerged from some
gloom and she is determined not to let it get the better
of her; still it lurks there, just at her heel.

I am sorry to run on so, my darling. You will accuse
me of projecting drama onto my colourless little life.
I think I hear Robin stirring—he at least was restful
after his episode of 'night' terrors. I must have Mrs O
prepare him some nourishment. Until later, my love—

I trust you will not be cross that I have lent some
of your older clothes to Robin. The clothes he arrived
in were quite beyond salvaging, and the few items
of apparel in his duffel were little more than tattered
rags. There is a trunk coming from Hastings, perhaps,
which may contain some clothing. I must say 'perhaps'
and 'may' due to its being quite difficult to extract any
certain intelligence—and I did come to feel like my
brother's enquisitor; as soon as I realised it, I refrained
from further questioning as I did not want Robin to
feel the target of intrusive investigation.

Let me take a few steps backward, my dear. It was
nearly the hour of noon when I heard Robin upon the
stair and I went to him straight away. Mrs O and I
had been listening for him, or for another episode, all
morning, and she was prepared to execute his breakfast as soon as he had roused. Robin sat upon the
fourth stair as if he could go no farther without risk of
faltering altogether. He had managed himself into his
threadbare pants in addition to his nightshirt, but his
feet were bare, and I had to resist the repulsion I felt

at the sight of them: ashen grey, with dirt I suppose,
and missing toes, his three smallest toes, one from his
left foot, two from his right. 'You must be famished',
I managed. 'Let me help you to your room, and Mrs
O'Hair will bring you some tea and food momentarily'.
Mrs O carried him up a pot of tea and toasted bread
with her currant jam. I can tell she is a trifle wary of
him, though she has not said as much. If she knew
him as I do, if she had known him in childhood and
his exuberant youth—then she could have no trepidation whatsoever. For Robin was the most assiduous,
studious and kindhearted boy, though solitary I must
acknowledge, especially in his youth, spending hour
upon hour in Uncle's library, reading and forming
(apparently) his design to explore the Arctic region.
To place his name alongside Magellan, Columbus, de
Soto. He would have liked to go to school, would have
liked to in the worst way, but of course that was not
possible—I know, my darling, I need not remind you;
you married a dowerless girl.

   To return to events: After a time, Mrs O retrieved
the teapot and such from Robin's room—he had drunk
every drop of tea but barely tasted the toast and jam.
It was then that Mrs O suggested that 'Master Robert
may like a bath, mum', and she was quite right to suggest it. She began heating water while I went upstairs
to broach the topic with Robin, who was at first reluctant but on account, I came to discover, of his having
no decent clothes afterward in which to dress. So I resolved that the only answer was for Robin to borrow

some of your things, my dear—again, I hope you shall
not object. I selected the items which I believe you
consider your least favored, which is why you left them
when you went on your business affair. Robin emerged
from his room having to keep hold of the pants, they
were so large upon his shrunken frame, and the shirt
hung like a sail on the mast of a becalmed ship. I had
no true idea of his thinness until I saw him in your
clothes, you who has always been so lean, due to your
great love of walking. Robin has become as lean and
as wiry as one of those dogs who live in the streets,
hunting for scraps—and also as chary, I should say,
for my brother gives the impression of always being
on alert, of constantly glancing over his shoulder, or
rather, of constantly *wanting to*. The ill-fitting clothes
were sufficient for him to reach the washroom, where
Mrs O had drawn him a hot bath. While he soaked,
Mrs O made the clothing more serviceable, fashioning loops and a drawstring to cinch the waist of the
pants, and gathering the shirt into pleats in back with
some well-placed stitches—all quite clever really, and
done with unexpected speed, though her eyesight has
faltered over the years, she tells me, and she had to
squint at the close work of sewing.

Meanwhile, I recalled that Mr Smythe had some
knowledge of barbering, in his younger days, thus I
went across the alley and spoke with him; luckily his
gout was not so insufferable, and it afforded him an opportunity to exercise a skill that had long lay dormant.
He required a moment to ready himself but presently

he was at our door, shears and comb in hand. The irony struck me then: here he had come to tidy my brother's appearance, while Mr S has allowed his own to lapse in his widowhood and infirmity. His hoary hair has grown wild, and his white muttonchops quite cover his ears, while his brows are like the unfolded snowy wings of owlets above his eyes. To facilitate the barbering, we set a kitchen chair outside the alley door, and Mr S went to work. Felix and Agatha sat on the stoop fascinated by the transformation of their uncle as Mr Smythe deposited long gobbets of hair into the gutter. I checked his progress now and again, and I found the metamorphosis startling too . . . or perhaps increasingly unsettling would be a more apt characterization. For on the one hand, Mr Smythe's barbering definitely rendered Robin more presentable—he had looked the part of the ruffian and wharf-dweller—but that mask had been obscuring Robin's gaunt and haunted physiognomy. His hair and beard were trimmed and shaped for parlour society, yet he appeared a man whose parlour stories would be grim tales of tragedies barely survived. I believe even Mr S was taken aback at the face that emerged from the marble, as he chipped away with his sculpting shears. When he was nearly finished I told the children it was time to return to their studies, and they were decidedly pale. I was hoping, I suppose, that grooming my brother would assure them that we are hosting a quite civilised creature under our roof—for they barely knew their uncle prior to his expedition—however,

I cannot imagine what they think of him now. They always heard stories of their Uncle Robin, his Herculean feats of autodidacticism, sequestered in *our* uncle's library at Lytham House, teaching himself calculus, astronomy, geography, anatomy, and heaven only knows. I would often imagine him there, alone in the book-lined room, the meekest of fires to fend off the chill, solitary in the rambling house except for Uncle's ancient man, William, who tended to Robin's needs until he eventually signed onto the whaler, the *Molly O'Toole*, as a common sailor to learn seamanship firsthand, figuring that for some kinds of knowledge only the thing itself will do. That is to say, he could not learn to captain his own expeditionary ship by books alone.

I am so sorry, my darling—I know you are well-acquainted with your brother-in-law's biography, but it does me good to recount things, to reaffirm them in my memory. I feel at times that the past is slipping from me, that I am perhaps thinking of someone else's history—or not even a real person's, rather a character's I have read in some author's book, and it has taken hold of me so that I cannot separate it from my own life's narrative (you know how easily I can become lost in a book, quite to my shame, I must acknowledge—I know you think it a personal flaw, and I have been trying to exorcise it during your absence, one of several qualities of the newly improved me of which I believe you will approve upon your return, but I shall merely tease you with that flirtatious hint, to entice you to conclude your affairs as expeditiously as possible).

In spite of being a trifle shocked by Robin's wasted appearance, Mr Smythe, no doubt due to his own loneliness and generally kind nature, invited him to smoke a bowl of tobacco with him after he had had a chance to sup—'a fine Rajasthan cut', Mr S described it. I knew that Robin would decline, if for no other reason than he had never been attracted to tobacco—but he surprised me by accepting our neighbour's invitation. I realised that my brother has no doubt taken up many new occupations during his years at sea, occupations to fill the countless empty hours among the desolate waves and phantasmagoric bergs of ice.

My occupation seems to be letter-writing, if not this letter itself. I find I do not want to put aside the pen and tend to responsibilities. And when I do, when necessity insists, I find that I am thinking of writing, itching to return to it. I have heard stories of the opium fiends, the men (and women) who are possessed by a desire for the drug, no matter its deleterious qualities. I can now relate to that possession. Writing seems to have unlocked something in me. I can only pray that it will not prove as destructive as a burning thirst for the fruits of the poppy.

(I know I have not posted, but I find myself only partway down a page, thus, my dear, to avoid the waste . . .)

The aroma of Mr Smythe's Oriental tobacco wafted indoors as the kitchen windows were raised to let some air circulate. Mrs O and I were preparing vegetables to add to the simmering stock, whose richness competed with the bowls of tobacco. With the windows raised a quarter, between chops and scrapes of Mrs O's and my blades, I overheard the pipe-smokers' conversation. Mr S dominated the discussion (which I expected, given my brother's taciturnity since his return). Mr S had served King and country in the colonies, and he was relating a tale that he experienced 'in the wilds of Nova Scotia'. The Indians there—Mr S pronounced the tribe's name but I shall not attempt to spell it—had a legend of some beast that lived in the forest, some creature that walked upon two legs, like a man, and was even reported to speak the names of his victims before dispatching them most horrifically. Mr S acknowledged that he was yet a young man and still possessed of an overly romantic fancy, so he was prone to believe such tales more than he ought. He was assigned to escort a survey detail to Fort Sackville, which required a three days' hike through the woods. On the first day, light began to fade by midafternoon, so impenetrable were the woods and so far north. This particular band of Indians kept dogs, and when they made camp the dogs would place themselves about its perimeter. The ragtag assembly of His Majesty's foot-soldiers, surveyors, native guides, and a pair of French trappers who served as linguists settled in for the long arboreal night, building their cook fire, preparing food and tea, and unpacking their bedrolls. The moment darkness descended in total, the dogs—great furry creatures, said Mr S, some northern relation of

the English mastiff—they became on edge and watchful. Their wide, shaggy backsides shone in the golden
firelight as they sat upon their haunches and stared
ever so keenly into the blackness that surrounded
them. The soldiers and the trappers attempted to dis-
regard the dogs, who would emit every now and then
a low growl, but their Indian masters were most attune
to the dogs' behavior. The Indians were as quiet as Pu-
ritans at prayer, sipping their tea and keeping their
fingers only inches from their long-bladed knives and
war-hatchets. Mr S fell asleep, utterly exhausted from
the hike and the Frenchmen's homemade spirits that
they had packed—only to awake later to some sort of
disturbance. It was still the blackest hours of night,
and the Indians were fully alert, standing with backs
to one another, their weapons drawn. Their big dogs
were on their feet menacing the darkness with their
rumbling growls. Mr Smythe and the other soldiers
took up their muskets, not bothering to charge and
load them by diminished firelight but brandishing
their bayonets.

I must say, I was slow in my vegetable preparation
as I was enthralled by our neighbour's tale. I am afraid
that was the climax of it, however. The camp eventually settled—though no one returned to sleep, Mr S
assured my brother. There were some language barriers, but Mr S came to understand from the Indians,
filtered through the Frenchmen into broken English,
that they believed they had had an encounter with 'the
Hairy Man of the Forest'—the being who had plagued

their people for generations. They further believed it was only the presence of their powerful dogs that dissuaded the Hairy Man from entering their camp.

Mr S had been long of wind, and his story had taken some time to tell—but he had clearly reached its conclusion, and by conventional rules it was Robin's turn to respond in some verbal way. Yet a silence ensued. Even Mrs O was quiet at her chopping as she too must have been spellbound by our neighbour's narrative. From my vantage I could not quite see the interlocutors. However, if I looked through the window, toward the left, I could see their pipes' upward columns of smoke; and when a few seconds of long-enduring silence stretched itself out, I spied that Robin's column was behaving most queerly, rising in a zigzag pattern as if a writhing serpent of steam. I leaned so that I had a fuller view and I saw that Robin's hand which held the pipe was trembling rather violently. I hastened to exit the kitchen and as I did I heard Mr S questioning my brother as to his disposition. I was momentarily at Robin's side. How to describe him? As I have said, his hand trembled, yes, as did his entire body; or perhaps more accurately, his entire being—for one received the impression that even his soul vibrated with whatever had taken hold of him. He stared into the space before him but not seeing the doors and windows of the close-quartered houses, as tightly together as barrel staves, yet seeing something else, something terrible, for his brow was knit in a contortion of horror. I swear, his hair and beard, though now neatly trimmed, had turned a hoarier white, as if he had aged while sitting in the alley, smoking and listening to our neighbour's strange story. It may be that a pallor had come to his countenance, beneath the beard, and it had magnified the strands of white. It occurred to me that someone looking upon the scene may believe at a glance that Mr Smythe and Robin are contemporaries—yet my brother is but thirty years old. I considered for a moment that my arithmetic must be in error, he seemed so aged before my eyes there in the alley. The figure is quite correct, however.

Mr S removed the pipe from Robin's trembling grip (his fingers were solidly locked around the bowl), and I coaxed him to stand. It required a moment's urging but he did finally rise and allow me to assist him indoors. I thanked Mr S for his kindnesses, over my shoulder, and wished him a good evening. I believe he felt responsible as the instrument of Robin's petrification, but I did not believe him at fault. There is no question that Robin returned to us with a fragile constitution—Mr S could not have known that an interesting traveler's tale would have such an affect on Robin, himself now a man of the wide world. No doubt our neighbour was hoping to prompt Robin into sharing some intriguing narrative of his own journeys, tit for tat—something to bring some colour to Mr S's typically monochromatic day.

Robin's reaction recalled for me the behaviours of some of the men who fought against the colonies in their rebellion. I was still a girl when they began to

come home in their inglorious defeat. In particular I
recall the son of our neighbours, the Wadkinses. On
occasion he would accompany them when they came
for tea. Nathan was his name. I was permitted to sit
in the parlour as long as I did not speak. I remember
observing Mr Nathan, who also was largely taciturn
on these visitings, and it occurred to me there was
something rather *shattered* about him. Not his phy-
sique, I mean—although he did appear to favor one
leg—rather, his spirit or his *persona* was in pieces, like
a china platter that has been dropped, and it lay upon
the floor essentially in the pattern of its former self,
but the pieces are no longer connected and some are
angled oddly from the whole of the new composition,
and here and there some small fragments may seem to
be missing altogether. (There have been nights, when
I silently looked upon the children in their beds, that
I felt like such a platter, now that I conjure the comparison.)

So that is how I thought of Robin as I assisted him
indoors: He resembled his former self, but there was
something broken about him. I do not want to alarm
you, my dear; Robin is not violent, I am certain of it.
Beneath whatever has affected him so profoundly,
he is still the gentle, kindhearted brother whom I remember so fondly. And, to be sure, once he was seated
in our cozy parlour, with a shawl upon his shoulders,
though it was to ward off a chill that only he seemed
to feel, and with a cup of Mrs O's excellent tea—Robin
became at peace again.

Here I have been filling sheet upon sheet with my rambling thoughts and observations, and have said very little of our dear ones, about whom, I know, you thirst for intelligences most of all! I have mentioned how I believe you will take to the industrious Mrs O'Hair—well, certainly Agatha has. I often find her spying Mrs O from the hall or through the window, when she and her brother are to be playing out-of-doors to receive some air. Aggie seems most fascinated with the exotic Mrs O. Neither of the children has been much exposed to the Irish, particularly an Irish*woman*. Of course Mrs O was not blind to Aggie's fascination, and she began inviting her to assist her in her duties, especially in the kitchen, for Agatha's edification—not to train our little girl to be a domestic! Of course not. But there are certain fundamental skills that are useful to possess no matter one's station in life. I am certain, my dear, that you agree on that point. For how can one evaluate a cook's or a maid's skillfulness if one has no base of knowledge from which to judge? I have always felt somewhat off my footing in such matters, relying principally on luck when employing necessary positions. Which is why I have availed myself of Mrs O's clear expertises; and I, also, am being tutored, though not as directly as our Agatha. As I sit and stitch in the kitchen, I keep a keen eye on Mrs O's procedures, committing them to memory until such time that I may record them in my miscellany. Except of course for those times I have been pointedly involved, as in the making of the currant jam.

At first Mrs O was loath to afford Aggie much responsibility, undoubtedly feeling that she was too
much of a child—she presents that image on account
of her being small for her age. But Mrs O has come
to accept that our Agatha is twelve, or nearly so, and
hence is become a young lady. I daresay she will be
out and married and raising a family of her own before we know what has happened. Though I must say
it is difficult to imagine at times; when, for instance,
she and Felix play knucklebones or nine-men's-Morris
in the alley; or when she carries with her on stormy
nights Miss Buzzle, her ragdoll; or when she and Felix
squabble over the most childish disputes, like who will
receive the last bit of ice shavings to sweeten with molasses (you will recall what a treat the children count
it, especially our little Maurice, who seemed to have a
molasses tooth).

Do not mistake me: The children are good. You
can be proud of them in your absence. As I said, Agatha is become a young lady. When she assists Mrs
O in the kitchen, she pins up her hair into a chestnut
bun, and she dons an apron that Mrs O has fashioned
just her size; add the air of seriousness, and our Aggie could pass for mistress of her own house. I was
struck with that image, again, just the other day, the
day before Robin's arrival, I believe. I said something
in greeting when I entered the kitchen, and Aggie
turned to me and there was a thumbprint of flour on
her cheekbone; and something about it along with her
hair swept from her face (classically heart-shaped, as

you always said), and maybe, too, the grey shade of her frock's collar—well, I was struck by the blue of her eyes. I remembered thinking of them as 'glacial' blue, which was odd for I have never been in the far northern part of the world, and I surmised it was an adjective I must have extracted from one of Robin's letters, though I could not recall the phrase's origin precisely. I thought that I must take up my brother's correspondences from the bureau drawer in the parlour, and re-read them to satisfy my curiosity about the word in my vocabulary—for it may have gained entrance from some other source, from some book, for example.

However, then I neglected to take up the letters, and the very next day Robin turned up in our foyer, as reborn as Lazarus. And Robin's eyes, too, exhibited the exact icy-blue quality of Agatha's—I take note of the similarity only now, in retrospect.

(I must cease for the time being, dearest, and I could justify posting, for I have very nearly reached the terminus of this sheet—but I feel I must give Felix, out of maternal fairness, equal 'stage time', as it were.)

Sept 7—I believe the greatest change you will discover in Felix when you return is his bibliophilism. He always enjoyed being read to but in the past few months his own passion for reading has become inflamed. Even when he is at play with his sister, in the alley or hall or parlour, he likes to have a book near at hand, almost as if comforted by it, the way Miss Buzzle comforts Agatha. I know you at times felt entombed by Uncle's books when they arrived in two full

carts and we had no choice but to stack them along
the walls in every room, save the kitchen and washroom, for the modest bookcase in the parlour could
hold but a thimbleful compared to the tun that would
be required. I further know your sometimes irksome
disposition toward the stacks of books that haunt
about the house was due to your disappointment in
the settling of Uncle's estate, but it is fortunate that
Uncle bequeathed a significant portion of his library
to me—largely books of poetry and romances—and
not simply left everything to Robin, who surely would
have liquidated the books along with everything else
to finance his expedition; and they would be gone now
too. The *Benjamin Franklin* must remain, yet I fear she
may be in as sad a state as her master, in which case
she can only be auctioned in sections for her timber,
and whichever gear survived. As you may surmise, I
have not broached such subjects with my brother.

There is a trader in books in Marchmont Street, you
may recall, Mr Squire, and of late I have sold a volume
or two. I must be watchful of course not to dispose of
one of Felix's favorites, the Sarah Fielding, for instance,
or the John Gays, or the American author, Mr Irving.
I wonder sometimes at Uncle's tastes. Perhaps he was
indiscriminate and purchased books as much for their
mere availability as for their subject matter. Felix may
have inherited the trait as his selections of material are
remarkably eclectic; for a day or two favoring a novel,
then a collection of verse, then drama. Oftentimes he
is so ardent in his reading I am reluctant to force him

to move on to other studies of a morning—yet I know how earnest you are to have him learn his figures, and geography.

At present Felix is engaged in the *Beggar's Opera*. His favored place is in the corner of the kitchen nearest to the washroom door, and next to a window of course. Mrs O'Hair will fix him his tea, with a splash of milk, as he prefers, and set it on the sill within easy reach from his chair. He will have rolled up the rug as a cushion for his feet, and if it is an especially drafty morning he will place one of my shawls over his shoulders. He will then appear quite the little man, with his old book and tea and shawl. All he would require is a pipe to complete the tableau. Of course his hair hanging down and the perfect ivory of his hands and face falsify the impression. Mrs O's pet-name for Felix is 'Old Soul'.

I am most definitely posting this letter today—this very moment in fact!

I miss you terribly, my dear, and I trust that your business will conclude soon and you will return to us.

Yours

Forever,

September 8, 18—

Dear Philip,

No doubt due to my brother's sudden return to our lives, I find myself more and more borne back to the days of childhood, to a time before my father's passing. One would think it a halcyon period, especially in comparison to the period after Papa's death—but the utter chaos of that time seems largely expunged from my memory. I was a girl; then Papa became ill with pneumonia after being caught in the terrible storm returning from Hampstead; then there was his funeral (nothing remains but impressions of blackness); then there is the period which is all but disappeared—when we were uprooted, like weeds from the garden, and relocated to become Uncle's dependents, phantasmal years, banked in fog.

It is the years before all of that which have been returning to me so vividly. The years when Robin was at my heel more often than not, like a devoted terrier, ready to engage in whatever game was my wish of the moment. We would fashion a corner of the arcade into a cottage of my own, the parameters established via well-positioned chairs and a blanket hung from the hooks normally used for baskets of flowers and herbs; there, I would play at being mistress, and my solitary guest for tea would be Robin—for tea, for cribbage, for the cutting of paper ornaments . . . for whatever suited me. My minion, two years my junior, was game for whatever amusement I chose. One day, it was late autumn and the weather was near to giving up its ghost to winter. A cold slashing wind made us abandon my 'cottage'; it upended a chair and blew from the table where I held court the playing cards I was using to tell our fortunes. Unpracticed gypsy that I was, I had no foretelling of this being our final such party. He would turn to more boyish pursuits, often more solitary pursuits—which held no room for his elder sister. Such would be my pattern on that icy autumn day, as rain blew inward the soaked blanket which was supposed to shield us from cold calamity; I would not recognise a loss upon its earliest introduction, but only in retrospection could I make out the figure of Finality, the figure of Parting, as if they stood by obscured in a grey gloom.

Robin was reluctant to return indoors even though our play area had been blown asunder. He seemed to be enthralled by the whipping wind and piercing pricks of rain. Could the seed have been sown that day? The kernel which grew into his obsession with

the northern pole? I can only now wonder. I took him
by the arm to urge him from the porch, and his skin
was as cold as the pump-handle in winter, and slick
with water too. I had the oddest notion—why I should
recall it all these years hence?—that my fingers may
freeze to my brother's ice-cold arm. The irony is that
that day seemed, looking back, to mark a kind of separation between us. By the following spring, Robin
had become more independent in his occupations, no
longer content to be my devoted playmate. One of the
telltale signs was that his name for me changed too. I
had time *in memoriam* been 'Magpie' on his childish
lips; sometime that winter I became merely 'Margaret'—the name by which everyone called me. Robin
and I had lost our avian kinship. He, meanwhile, began encouraging the use of his true Christian name. I
was alone in my recalcitrance, clinging to the familiar
name of his childhood. As I obviously do still.

Listen to me! Waxing with these long-ago memories. Robin's return has indeed broke loose a torrent of
recollections, embrined with all manner of conjured
meanings and emotions; and it seems my only egress
for them lies in inditement: I am compelled to pay
them out across the page in a tangled line of script.

Thank you for indulging me, my dear.

I have returned, it is still a goodly amount of time
before dawn. I feel wasteful of the candle, but there is
no returning to sleep, as I experience a nervousness
which prevents me from resting quietly until sun-
rise. I woke in the night and was of a mind to look in

on the children when I heard footsteps in the hall; I glanced toward my door just as a light retreated beneath it. I imagined it was Robin. After a moment I rose and donned my robe; I did not bother with a light of my own. As I entered the hall I heard the front door shut. As soon as I reached the bottom step of the stair I detected the scent of a snuffed flame. The candle in its holder was on the foyer table, and Robin was not about. He must have needed the night air, I determined at first, still thinking of him in the terms of a boy—but I instantly amended myself. Robin is a grown man, a seasoned sailor in fact. Pardon my coarseness, my dear, but I could imagine that Robin felt the need for something more than night air. He would not need to travel far afield. Our section of the city, like every other perhaps, is teeming with such ... attractions.

I find I cannot fault him, for loneliness is a hard master, inflicting his lashes most vigorously during the quietest moments. Yet there will also be a sting, sharp and sudden, amid the most frenetic commotion. There was an instance of loneliness's surprising strike on the morning of Robin's arrival. Mrs O and I were busy at boiling the currant berries—she had been instructing me how best to detect when the berries are just the proper texture, and the children were having an animated disagreement in regards to the construction methods of the Great Pyramids (their history lesson on that morning)—when, rather like a spasm of electricity, I felt the kiss of loneliness's lash upon my soul. Then, for a moment, it was as if I were under water, and all the sounds of the kitchen—the hissing water of the boiling pot, the stove-door's protesting hinge as Mrs O stirred the fire, the children's pitching voices—they were all muted and far away. I could only clutch at the knots of my apron and wait for the despairing pang to wash over me and, then, recede. It was not long after that Aggie broke the bowl and Robin arrived.

I hope, my darling, that you are not so troubled with loneliness, and that you have amiable companions at your lodging and among your business acquaintances. I trust that the landlady, Mrs Turnbull, looks after you as she would her own relation. Perhaps you would assure me of your comforts when you write, so that I may be certain you are not plagued by such pernicious cares.

Just as I have been describing myself as some castaway, cut off like Crusoe from human fellowship, I find I must describe an incident much to the children's benefits which is owed to Mr Smythe and Mrs O'Hair. When I was performing my toilet, the former brought to us a bundle of charcoal pencils, a dozen all tied together with crimson string. They are the sort that artists use, and where Mr S acquired them I cannot imagine. Nevertheless he delivered them to Mrs O, who immediately recognised their potential value to the children. A few minutes thereafter the butcher's fellow delivered the stew meat which Mrs O had ordered—and she pressed him for any spare scraps of butcher's paper he may have in his cart. He did indeed possess some odds and ends, cut at irregular angles, that he gave to her. So by the time I entered the kitchen both Felix and Agatha were at the table sketching pictures on the ragtag paper. They all could see that I was astonished—which amused the three of them exceedingly!—and forthwith Mrs O described the series of events that led to the surprising circumstance. For their having no formal training, I was pleased that the children's ardor was nearly matched by their skills. Aggie was engaged in a mind's-eye portrait of the calico cat ('Patches' the children have dubbed her) who comes round the alley hunting mice and kindly laid saucers of milk. It seemed to me that Aggie had rendered the feline's legs too short but had captured the shape and angle of her ears just so. Felix, meanwhile, was at work on a scene which did not at first come to me, two fellows and a young woman; but the iron-barred window in the background shed light upon the trio. They must be Macheath, Lockit, and Polly Peachum (from the *Beggar's Opera*). What a funny young man, our Felix, to be so taken by such a work. Why not knights and dragons? Or something of a biblical bent . . . Samson in chains, Daniel in the den of lions? Or tri-headed Cerberus? Talon-tortured Prometheus bound to his boulder?

I, of course, complimented the artists on their masterpieces, for I was truly impressed. Shortly I heard the front door, and it was Robin returning from his night's haunting. I went to the hall to speak with

him—though about what precisely, I know not—
however, he and I stood stopped, facing one another
for several moments, saying nothing. He looked the
fellow who had spent a long night. Dark semicircles
drooped beneath his eyes, underscoring the paleness
of the surrounding skin—and in the midst of these
pools of pure exhaustion floated the ice-encased eyes
of frozen blue. Robin was somewhat stooped, as if too
tired to stand fully erect. He and I exchanged not a
syllable, but I am not certain if it was a silence of utter
understanding or one of complete incomprehension.
Could it be both?

I smelt no liquor on him, nor tobacco, nor any other
scents which would lead one to conclude he had spent
an evening of carousing and debauchery—yet Robin's
exhaustion was beyond doubt. After another moment
he initiated his trudging ascent, and then disappeared
into his room. We did not hear from him for the remainder of the day.

Watching his weary body move from one step to
the next with such deliberate effort, it came to me that
I have not enquired of Robin's success (or failure) in
his mission to reach the northern pole. His condition
upon his arrival here—and his defeated and beaten
demeanor since—would lead one to infer abject failure. Additionally, if he had succeeded, would not Robin be hailed the conquering hero? Would there not be
dignitaries of the maritime and geographic societies
queuing up at our door? Would not the bells of London peal the momentous event? Yet, still, how near

did my brother come to the goal? What obstacles did he overcome along the journey (for there must have been many)? Which ones undid him and his hopes? But attempting and surviving so awesome of a feat—is that not cause enough for celebration? Is that not itself an awesome feat?

Robin possessed so many worthy ambitions: To solve the mystery of magnetism; to chart a northern passage to the Orient; to discover new species of flora and fauna adapted to the extreme cold and general hostility of the environment; and to tread where no man had before set foot. I recall with perfect clarity Robin's outlining of them to us the evening before he set sail. He was positively aglow! Equal parts golden lamplight, aged brandy, and unbounded enthusiasm for the commencement of a voyage so long in planning and preparation.

It is difficult to reconcile that fellow, in a private room of the Albatross Tavern in Hastings, with this one, so defeated and downtrodden. I must gain some intelligences regarding the expedition, and surely, hence, some of its successes. Yet I do not want Robin to feel the target of a hostile interrogation, as if hauled before the Maritime Board, designed to find fault and lay blame. . . .

I must leave off for now, my dearest. Aggie is calling for me.

Though we are a fractured family in your absence, Philip, I do feel that you would approve of the domestic scene which we managed to effect this evening.

Mrs O had prepared a late-garden cowcumber salad along with savory parsnip stew, though it was on the thin side, and I was able to coax Robin into joining us. I do believe he slept soundly for the remainder of the daylight hours; thus when we sat down to our homely repast, he appeared much improved. I know it is unorthodox, but I have developed the habit of allowing Mrs O to sit with us at table. It seems so unnecessary to trouble to set up the hinged table in the washroom, just to have Mrs O dine alone—I believe it was a different matter when you were home, and we had a cook as well as a paid girl: the pair of them taking meals together did not make the washroom dining seem so sterile and austere. Then Mrs Walcott gave notice, as did Sally shortly thereafter—and we were left in an awkward circumstance. Fortunately, as you know, Mrs O'Hair was found in short order, on the good knowledge of Mr Smythe. At first, I had Mrs O continue the practice of taking her meals alone, but after a time it seemed a bit silly—and, besides, I missed having an adult with whom to converse lightly at luncheon or dinner; in truth, I have found Mrs O a surprisingly able conversationalist, for an Irishwoman. Tales from her childhood and descriptions of her people's strange ways have enlightened many a dark hour. (Do not fear, my dear, if you prefer to return to the practice of Mrs O's dining in the washroom, it will be quite understandable.)

To rejoin my main object: the little domestic scene. The table felt pleasantly full with the children on one side, Mrs O on the other, and Robin and I filling the head and foot. We were all quiet for a time, feeling somewhat unnatural at first, and occupied with passing the biscuit plate and the jam jar and such. As we were all just settled (and I was thinking what to say—imagine, I, lost for words), it was Robin, paradoxically, who initiated conversation, enquiring, 'Are these the artists'? meaning of course Felix and Aggie. He must have seen their sketches on the table in the foyer. 'I am most impressed', Robin said. You can imagine how the children beamed. 'They must have had a tutor', he said to me, taking up his spoon. 'No, none—only what I have been able to teach them. You will recall my interest in art, when we were children'. He appeared somewhat baffled by my remark; I wondered then if he recalled our childhoods at all. 'We had a man on the *Franklin*, our second steerman, who was a talented artist, had studied for a time in Berlin, but circumstances drove him to sea'. 'You had some natural talent', I reminded him, 'when we were children'. 'Did I'? 'Yes, indeed. In fact I remember a sketch of Max, our shepherd, that you rendered quite skillfully, given the age of your hand. I suppose you do not recall Maximus; he slept at the foot of your bed for years'. My brother chewed his food thoughtfully. 'I recall Max, certainly, but I am not certain of the sketch. I shall accept your word for it, dear sister'. He returned his attention to the children, enquiring of their interests and their ages (he had lost track during his years at sea). The children, as you may imagine, gobbled down the attention with more gusto than Mrs O's brothy stew. Robin's animation was heartening; yet I wondered at his line: Did he question the children so thoroughly to diminish my opportunity to question *him*? Perhaps I was reading too much into his attitude. In any event, it was a nicely domestic scene, and overall a balm of tranquility. I had good reason to hope for my brother's full recovery. The only small blight was Felix's fascination with Robin's missing fingers, which were conspicuous in their absence since he ate with a spoon in his remaining digits. There was no mistaking the object of Felix's attention as Robin would bring each spoonful of stew to his mouth. I was mildly anxious that Felix may make an enquiry as to the loss of them; but he did not. Surely Robin took note of Felix's fixed gaze; however, he volunteered nothing. Perhaps he felt the topic to be uncouth for the dinnertable.

Earlier, Mrs O had shown Aggie how to bake slices of bread softened with a few drops of cream and sprinkled with cinnamon and sugar—she called them 'faerie scones'; and when we were finished with our stew, Aggie proudly retrieved the tray of treats, where they remained warm atop the stove, and brought them to table. We filled our cups with fresh tea, and Robin, as guest of honor, was prevailed upon to sample the inaugural scone. We watched expectantly as he took a bite—and instantly aimed a look of approval at the anxious Agatha: 'Most excellent', he declared, chewing and savoring. As you may imagine, the neophyte cook nearly expired of joy.

Look at the time! I must extinguish the candle, my dear, and retire. There is little more to relate of our evening. After dinner, Robin went to his room and was not heard from thereafter. My suspicion is that he availed himself of one of the many volumes in the chamber and read by lamplight. Oh, that you were here to warm our bed, dear husband!

Sept 9—Greetings again, my dear. We have just concluded a visit from the oddest little fellow, a Mr Havens, of the Geographic Society, an undersecretary of some sort, coming to call on Robin. At first, it seemed he was come on behalf of the Society, but I half suspect that he was more representative of his own designs. He arrived at our door at quarter past ten; Robin had only just risen and taken his tea. Felix opened the door, for Mrs O and I were engaged in the kitchen. I discovered Robin had a caller when Felix was at my elbow proffering a card. I had Felix install the new arrival to the parlour whilst I went to the alley to alert Robin, who had taken out a chair and was reading. Robin's reluctance was clear but in a moment we were seated with Mr Havens. What an odd-looking man. He wears an especially high collar and a long coat—I imagine in the hopes that it all lends him the illusion of height. In fact, the impression is just the contrary, as he seems to have *fallen in* to his apparel and may require some assistance in climbing out. Bushy brows, a pencil-thin nose, and full (nearly Negroid) lips show in the recess of his starched collar. He began by making certain that Robin was indeed

master of the *Benjamin Franklin*—perhaps his makeshift clothes and worn-thin condition did not present
the expected image of ship's captain, of Arctic explorer. Once reassured, Mr Havens began asking Robin
about the particulars of his adventure, and I thought,
'How fortuitous; I have been wanting to gain such intelligences and now our strange little guest can act as
the instrument of their extraction'. Or so I believed at
first—however, it soon became clear that Robin was
unwilling to divulge much to his enquisitor, especially
in terms of specific details. He confirmed his essential
route—through the Norwayan and Barents Seas—and
his essential objects—the root cause of magnetism,
etc., etc.—but beyond that already familiar terrain,
Mr Havens's own explorations were inconsequential.
Robin deflected his interrogatories with consistently
cryptic and vague responses. Eventually Mr Havens
decided upon a new stratagem (Mrs O had brought us
tea, and for a long moment the Society's undersecretary held his cup and peered at the surface of his liba-
tion, as if answers to his queries may be found among
its beclouded surface). He said that a paper for the Society's journal would be most valuable; then Mr Havens entered into such circumlocutions that I was not
entirely certain at what he was aiming—that a book,
presumably about Robin's explorations (in addition to
?, in lieu of ? the aforementioned paper) may be even
more valuable—however, such a book would not be
published by the Geographic Society, but rather via a
private firm, and Mr Havens seemed to be offering his

services as agent . . . something to that effect. I noticed that as soon as Mr Havens embarked upon the topic of a book, Robin began to grow uneasy. I feared he was entering into a state akin to the one Mr Smythe's traveler's tale delivered him. The difficulty I experienced attempting to decipher the undersecretary's design was exacerbated by my maintaining part of my attention on my brother, watching for signs of his slipping further along the sickly track.

Robin kept hold of his equanimity—though my perception was that it took considerable effort—and finally we were able to extricate ourselves from Mr Havens's company; I expressed our appreciation for his visiting and assured him that Robin would consider all that he had intimated (I did not mention that chief among the goals of consideration was determining precisely what the odd fellow had proposed). I thought that perhaps Robin and I may begin such consideration as soon as our guest departed; instead, my brother returned to his book in the alley, though the day was donning grey and whispering the possibility of rain.

The following morning, *Sept 10*—It is unlikely, any longer, to sleep so soundly through the night, but I did so. I believe my sleeping has been so poor for so long that utter exhaustion at last caught me up, and did me a good turn. As I was dressing I realised I knew not whether my brother was in his room or out on another ramble. When I stepped into the hall I listened at his door but heard nothing. Even if he had been muttering in tongues it would have been a relief (of sorts). Downstairs, Mrs O was already at work mixing the ingredients for biscuits. She had only got a pan of them in the oven when Felix, our early riser, appeared in the kitchen, his hair still needing a thorough wetting and combing; and he had a most perplexed countenance. I was cracking eggs in a bowl for Mrs O to scramble, with a pinch of salt and dried onion. I asked Felix what the matter was, and he asked us if we had taken any paper or a pencil. Upon waking he had gone directly to the table in the parlour where we had selected to store the art supplies; and he was convinced it had been depleted. Perhaps he had merely lost count, I proposed (though I know that would not be like our Felix, who has many of the business traits of his father). However, he was adamant that he had known the precise number when he retired. To his credit, Felix was not displaying childish pique but was nevertheless resolute on the matter. I assured him that I would reach the bottom of the subject, and he went about his morning ablutions. In a few minutes Agatha was downstairs, and Mrs O was setting out breakfast.

Still, my curiosity about the paper and pencil clung tenaciously; and at my earliest opportunity I absconded upstairs: Mrs O and the children were thoroughly engaged in their respective tasks, and had no thought of my whereabouts. In the hall I at first went to my door, even masking from myself my true design. I stood with my hand upon the knob listening for sounds from Robin's room; there was none. I thought perhaps, then, he had slipped from the house. I waited before his closed door for a full minute or more. I cautiously took hold of the knob, turned it, and stepped through an opening just wide enough. The room was dim so I hesitated a moment to allow my sight to compensate. Daylight lingered at the edges of the curtained window like a narrow frame about a picture, broken here and there. Robin's dark shape became discernible on the bed. The impression was that he was dead asleep. My velvet-shod feet disturbed the stillness of the room but little. I went directly to Maurice's desk, still set in the corner of the room, and I recognised the odd shapes of the butcher's paper, and the silhouette of a charcoal pencil, greatly reduced from use. There seemed to be images on the paper but the light was too poor to make them out. I looked back at Robin, who lay upon his side, his position unchanged; the form of the blankets hid his face. I quietly took up the paper, two irregular sheets; and stepped to the window. Holding the paper close to the wall and using the weakly narrow beams that crept into the gloom, I surveyed the images that Robin had drawn there.

The first was a portrait of a handsome though haggard man. My first impression was that Robin's unpracticed hand skewed the proportions and the subject's eyes were too large; however, soon a second idea came to me: the eyes were not overlarge but rather they suggested the same haunted expression of Robin's orbs. They were of course in charcoal grey but I surmised if Robin could have rendered them in full palette, the eyes would have been in the same glacial blue as his own, lending them an air of frigid isolation. The man in the portrait had an unkempt beard, again, not unlike Robin's when he first arrived, and he wore a fur collar about his neck. The fur was here and there matted or missing in an odd patch. It was the portrait of a wretched fellow who had been through a hellscape of ice.

I examined the other piece of paper to discover a more astonishing—and disturbing!—image: Also the portrait of a man, I suppose (it may be some manner of beast), but in three-quarter profile and nearly a full body's rendering. The being's hair was long and black and flowing, caught in the polar wind. It is glancing back, at the artist's perspective; and even in partial profile, how to describe the look? It was a look of menace certainly—but yet so much more, too. It is astonishing that Robin's inexpert hand could communicate so much regarding the being—perhaps a testament to the profundity of its impact on his mind, on his soul. The being's gaunt, hairless cheeks, with darkened lips drawn in a sneer, provokes a sudden terror in the viewer, but then almost instantly, perhaps after the initial shock has washed over, one senses that the terror is also felt by the being—as when a wild animal is cornered by hunters and it is both terri*fying* and terri*fied*. That realization prompted me to refocus my attention to the being's eye, and in its frozen, cadaverous attitude there was (unnoticed before) the echoes of pain and fear. And I knew these echoes are in Robin's eyes as well. How could I, his only surviving family, not have seen them until now, reflected in the portrait of this polar inhabitant?

I felt my cheeks dampen. I replaced the sketches to Maurice's desk, and I blotted at my eyes with the sleeve of my blouse. I turned to look upon whom I had wronged and was startled to realise Robin was awake and looking at me; he had been silently observing as I snooped at his drawings. The profound sympathy I had felt only a moment before transformed into profound shame at my invasion of Robin's privacy, and not simply the privacy of his room; rather, the privacy of his past, of his memories, of his very being. Perhaps my brother felt sympathy for me, too, in being caught so compromised. We peered at one another a long moment—then Agatha called for me from the foot of the stairs; I cast my eyes down and hurried from the room, which Robin's and my mutual muteness filled like a stifling gas.

The images have stayed with me throughout the day, like images from a fretful dream that remain to oppress long after waking. I think, too, of the Hairy Man from Mr Smythe's haunting tale. The images bizarrely bind together as if they wish to blend into a single being.

I was going to post this letter, my dear, but quite out of the blue Mr Smythe has extended an invitation to Robin and me for tea at his rooms this very evening—'on the occasion of becoming acquainted with new residents of Marchmont Street' the invitation reads in Mr S's crawling script. I must hold the letter until I may add report of this most unexpected development—it will perhaps afford an amusing closure to an otherwise troubling narration.

Amusing indeed, my dear. Robin and I were introduced to the most intriguing couple, but more of them in a moment. When Robin emerged from his room, about two hours after my discovery of his artwork, and he learned of Mr S's invitation, he was not immediately agreeable, protesting at first that his makeshift wardrobe was insufficient for the occasion. That proved to be a minor obstacle, what with the remaining items of yours and the clever Mrs O'Hair. You may recall your green wool waistcoat, with the brass buttons. More of Mrs O's ingenious pleating, along the sides, and the old waistcoat was most serviceable. We added your dark blue neckcloth, craveted in solitaire fashion, and Robin was more than presentable to come calling for tea. With objections over apparel removed, Robin had to acquiesce. Who knows, by getting out and about (in polite company) Robin may make acquaintance which leads to a position. Of course I made no mention of that prospect; I do not want Robin to feel that he is a burden. Felix and Agatha were somewhat sullen because they were not included in Mr S's invitation, but Mrs O brightened their moods with the promise of teaching them a game from her youth, 'beggar with the button', she called it.

Thus there was domestic harmony when Robin and I ventured across the alley at about four o'clock to call at Mr Smythe's. I had forgotten how much potential for airiness Mr S's rooms possessed, but was unrealised due to the tightly arranged furniture, all a bit oversized, and the heavy draperies. Even the wall art, thickly framed paintings of densely packed crowds, contribute to a claustrophobic sense. However, one could tell Mr S had tidied and primped for the occasion, in addition to doing his best to domesticate his own appearance. He had donned a jacket of regimental red with large, polished buttons (though I doubt the jacket would actually button if called to the task); and a wide, drooping tie of watchman wool was knotted securely at his neck. Mr S ushered us into the packed parlour, a room of next to no floor space but abundant seating, as long as one does not object to the intimacies of knees and elbows sometimes brushing.

Robin and I had just settled onto a low horsehair sofa, and Mr S was retrieving a plate of sweets to offer us, when the door chimed with the other guests' arrival. In a moment our host was introducing a quite striking young couple, Mr and Mrs Shelley—he could not have been much beyond his early twenties, and she perhaps still in her teens. Mr Shelley's charming qualities were immediately apparent, with his blue eyes, sandy locks, and almost feminine cheekbones. He had something of the look of a Roman deity. After a time I decided that the prominence of his cheekbones, in fact all the angularness of his features, was due to his thinness, a thinness which was approaching emaciation. His coat hung loosely about his narrow

shoulders. As distinctive as Mr Shelley's appearance
was, it was his wife who tended to command one's eye.
To describe her, you would find her quite ordinary—
light though lusterless hair which she had attempted
to style becomingly, but it emerged as part bun and
part half-formed ringlets framing her pale face. Her
eyes, too, were dull. Yet she exerted a strange magnetism. Her look and demeanor intimated that she was
the survivor of some terrible shipwreck, that she had
come through contrary to the odds, which had been
set firmly against her. Though she spoke not of any
such event, and it was in her speaking that one could
comprehend the affinity between husband and wife.

It seemed that Mr S had met them at the bookshop
on Marchmont Street. The butcher's fellow had very
kindly conveyed our neighbour there in his cart, aware
of the bothersomeness of Mr S's gout. Our neighbour
was hoping to acquire some new reading material in
trade. He was letting go of a volume on the Roman
catacombs, nicely bound and gilt-edged. He was hoping to barter at a one-to-three ratio, he said, or at least
one-to-two. He discovered Mr Squire the shopkeeper
in conversation with this young couple, just returned
to England from the Continent. They had brought in
a volume of German folktales, in Deutsch, and a miscellany of wineshops in Montparnasse. Mr Squire appeared in an especially cantankerous mood and would
not barter but offered a few pennies to purchase them.
A history of Pompeii and something about highway-
men of the Italian Alps had struck their fancies—but

Mr Squire would not part with them in trade. Mr Smythe, who had taken a chair in the corner of the old shop to await an audience with its capricious keeper, noted the Italian flavoring of the books the young couple had spied, and spoke up, perhaps out of turn, offering his catacombs book for their Bavarian tales—a direct exchange bypassing Mr Squire altogether—and he further suggested that the shopkeeper's standing offer of a few pennies was more in line with the single volume on Montparnasse vintners, not for two nicely kept books. (At least this is how Mr S accounted the tale of their meeting, with himself playing the role of day-saving hero, and the young people, politely, did not contradict our host.)

Mr Squire agreed to the bargain, probably not especially interested in any of the titles in question. The young man introduced himself and his wife as Mr and Mrs Shelley, newly of Marchmont Street themselves. Mr Smythe indicated that he had more volumes that they may be interested in borrowing and invited them for tea upon the following afternoon. And there we all sat.

Robin had been the epitome of taciturnity since our arrival, holding his cup and saucer in his lap, not even bothering to sip at his tea, a fine Indian blend with a strong suggestion of orange blossom. Mrs Shelley spoke of their having returned from the Continent. They traveled with a small collection of books—'Alexandria' they called it self-mockingly—which they read thoroughly and repeatedly but were now quite ready for fresh material. 'Particularly', added Mr Shelley, 'books having to do with Italy'. They had only just returned from Europe but were already contemplating a Roman holiday. I wanted to bring Robin into the conversation (I know it is unflattering egotism on my part, but I felt a mounting fear that this intriguing young couple, so well-read and so worldly, would think my brother a dullard and mentally deficient and furthermore conclude that it was a family trait)—so I thought if I broached the subject of Robin's travels, it may encourage him to reveal something of his adventure. In retrospect, perhaps that was as much my motivation—to finally gain some small intelligence of Robin's time at sea—as was defending the family capacity for intellect from unfair assessment. 'My brother has just returned from a three-year exploration, his inaugural captaincy'. 'How very fascinating', said Mrs Shelley, her eyes flashing with sincerity. The rules of polite conversation clearly called for Robin to join in with something about his destination, if only in the vaguest of terms, yet he remained quite mute. Sitting next to him, at such close quarters, I noticed the tea in his cup; its surface rippling ever so slightly, suggesting his hand or legs or perhaps his whole body had begun to tremble, almost imperceptibly.

Inexplicably, my dear, I persisted. 'Yes, he and his crew explored the polar regions.' 'My word, this is quite remarkable. Is it not, my love'? She addressed Mr Shelley of course, who seemed to be paying out attention only by half. 'Yes', he reiterated, 'quite remarkable'.

Robin, with great effort of control, placed his tea on a side-table cluttered with framed images and returned his hands to his knees, which were drawn up due to the short-legged sofa. I knew that he was trying to summon his nerves to submission. I searched for a way to bring the topic to a close that would not be totally graceless. 'Perhaps you will be able to read all about his experiences. A gentleman from the Geographical Society approached Robin on the subject of publishing his accounts'. 'How wonderful. Congratulations, Mr Walton—or rather, Captain Walton'. 'Thank you. I must beg your pardon. Please excuse me'. And Robin rose from his seat and exited Mr Smythe's with such haste that no one was able to say much in parting.

After an awkward silence, 'You must excuse my brother. He is only just returned and is recovering from exhaustion'. 'Of course', said Mrs Shelley. 'I understand perfectly', and she squeezed her husband's hand. Husband and wife were quite close on a mohair settee. A look came upon Mr Shelley's face, only for an instant and I could not quite interpret it—but it seemed to carry a hint of anguish. Or perhaps I was seeing an echo of my brother's physiognomy reflected in this young fellow's, an echo that had fallen across his features like a passing shadow.

I am sorry, my love. I am succumbing to my flaw and flair for melodrama. To conclude the episode, I lingered a bit longer at our neighbour's before returning. My brother's sudden exit dampened what otherwise may have been a festive evening, likely to

include Mr S's squeezing behind his ancient fortepia-
no and sharing some romantic ballads from his youth
(his playing is underpracticed but he does possess a
fine natural baritone). Robin, meanwhile, had sequestered himself in Maurice's room and we have neither
seen nor heard him since. I must post this wandering
epistle on the morrow. Hopefully we will receive a few
words from you, my dear. It has been so long and I
know the children would love a letter from their 'Papa'.

You have

All my

Love,

September 11, 18—

Dear Philip,

Spending time with the young married couple—she very young—seems to have dislodged recollections of us, my dear, from a darkened chamber of my memory. Last night I was dreaming of the recollections; then awoke and continued, without interruption, collecting them like pretty presents strewn along a great curving corridor—around each turn is another, and another. One was of the bemused glances we exchanged while taking our vows because of the vicar's whistling lisp, you and I on the brink of giggling and destroying the solemnity altogether. We had to look away from one another as the vicar twittered through his text. And there were the births of our three beloveds, and our great joy as each was born healthy and strong-lunged into the world. I recalled how the worry drained from your troubled brow at learning that we were fine, the new babe and I. Your great-aunt shepherdessed each child and delivered you the good news as you waited in the parlour with your cider and your papers. I lay exhausted in bed as you entered the room to meet the newest arrival. Your face was similar, my dear, on the day you returned home with news of your own: that Mr Pfender was promoting you to principal clerk of the northern accounts. What a time we had, the five of us, celebrating the recognition of your hard work!

However, as I lay lonely in our bed, with only the earliest workmen moving hushed in the dark street, other sorts of memories returned to me, too: black memories of Maurice and his empty bed and Reverend Grayling's inadequate words, nearly two years and I recall every slashing syllable, every flaying phrase; and your shattered countenance, a crystal platter broken asunder; and your packing for your business affair, not knowing the length of time you would be away from us—and your sudden silence, maintained these many weeks. I do not scold, my love, only express my worry. Each time the postman arrives I hold my breath in hopes that he is ending my fretting with only a few of your words saying that you are safe and making plans for your return. But not even the latter is necessary: only to know you are well, *that* simple intelligence would be more than enough to make me happy. I would be tempted to turn a girlish cartwheel in the hall!

Changing subject: Since returning from tea at Mr Smythe's I find myself thinking about the wife, Mrs Shelley—there is something quite magnetic about her.

In her presence one can hardly bring oneself to look away, to not stare at her, especially her eyes, whose hue registers somewhere twixt leaden grey and azure-an blue, something like the seawater caught in a tidal pool after a coastal storm. Though she was perfectly calm during our encounter at Mr S's I suspect those eyes could become quite tempestuous indeed—the young woman seems to possess such passion locked inside that pacific shell. That was my impression at least. I can hear you chiding me, Philip, for allowing my imagination to run, for claiming to understand things about Mrs Shelley that I could not reasonably deduce during such an abbreviated encounter. You would be right, of course; but I cannot keep from feeling confident, too, in my impressions. I shall do my best to keep in mind that they are only working hypotheses, mere assumptions. I will perhaps have opportunity to bolster or dismantle them as I have sent Mrs Shelley an invitation to tea—and to peruse our copious volumes to see if she may like to borrow one or two, as long as they are not among Felix's favorites.

I have been preparing for her visit; in fact, preparations are complete and they came to be so with relative ease in large part due to the industrious Mrs O, who, among other tasks, baked a batch of gooseberry pastries to serve with tea. I suspect you may disapprove, but I am allowing the children to join Mrs Shelley and me in the parlour. I cannot count on Robin's joining us—he has been particularly reclusive since returning from Mr Smythe's—and I have a feeling that Mrs Shelley will be more at ease with the children present. She is after all not much older than a child herself; and yet there is an independence to her spirit which I imagine could be a positive influence on the children, especially Aggie, who seems of an age to be in search of models. Perhaps that is why she has taken so to Mrs O'Hair. Moreover, it will perhaps make up for my not allowing them to attend Mr S's *soirée*. . . .

The children enjoyed appareling themselves for the grand event. Felix borrowed your cravat, the same that Robin wore, and he tied it in a similar, though unpracticed, fashion. It hung to his knee but he was visibly proud of its smartness, so I did not intercede to attempt a re-adjustment. Agatha wore her best frock, the pearl grey with the rose-pink bib. I braided her hair, which reaches her slender waist; and Mrs O unearthed a strand of red ribbon from somewhere with which she tied a complementary bow for Aggie's braid: *très chic*. Dressed so, it was not difficult to imagine our little girl as the mistress of her own house, a situation which will come about quicker than not.

We were expecting Mrs Shelley at 2 so when it became 3 I suspected the young woman was prevented from our appointment. Felix and Agatha were paragons of patience, he reading in the corner of the parlour, she hostessing her own tea with Miss Buzzle and her other dollies. Mrs. O taught Aggie how to cut patterns from paper and use them to make clothes for her dolls, thus they are colourfully appareled in simple clothing sewn from odds and ends. I was attempting to follow Felix's example and had selected a book of verse by Prior, *The Turtle and the Sparrow*; however, my mind was too full to focus on the poems for more than a stanza or two before wandering. That is more and more the way of it: I must remain busy every moment for the second I attempt to repose I begin to flutter through a kaleidoscope of cares. If I am assisting Mrs O in the kitchen and we are waiting for something to rise or to bake or to simmer, my mind immediately turns to some worrisome topic. If I am lucky, when I retire, I am so exhausted that I am able to fall asleep before my mind can engage such thoughts. These letters help to settle my turbulent head, in part because they contribute to my exhaustion. (I am sorry, my dear, for sidestepping onto this track. I shall return to describing the events of earlier in the hope that they may amuse you.)

As I said, I was quite at the point of conceding Mrs Shelley when there was a knock upon the door. Mrs O, who must have been listening for any sign of our guest's arrival like an Irish wolfhound, was at the door immediately and ushering Mrs Shelley to the parlour. She wore the same grey dress as she had worn to Mr S's, with the addition of a tartan wrap draped about her narrow shoulders and pinned at the left. There was something about the colourful accessory which magnified the crystalline quality of her eyes. I was reminded of the marble statuary at the National whose chiseled orbs are always quite vivid in their attitude, yet nevertheless made of stone—a fact the viewer is unable to overlook no matter how skilled the sculptor.

I greeted Mrs Shelley, who soon was asking that I call her by the familiar name of 'Mae, m-a-e' (May), and I introduced the children to her, inviting her to be seated on the mohair sofa. Momentarily Mrs O brought the tea and the little pastries she had prepared. It was a most congenial and cozy atmosphere. Due to the prominence of books in the room, not only filling the bookcases but stacked along the walls and sitting about here and there on the salon table and arms of chairs, et cetera; and of course Mae's ostensible reason for paying the visit—she right away began commenting on them and enquiring of the source. I told the tale of my uncle and my sole inheritance. Mae then related how her father is a writer as well as a publisher—and she mentioned her husband in a way that suggested I was already aware of his status as writer and poet. I did not desire to demonstrate my ignorance, nor to insult her if it were a case of a wife's assessment of her spouse's talents and reputation being intemperate; thus I was mainly taciturn on the subject, suggesting, I hoped, an air of recognition.

'My mother, too, was an author, as you may know', said Mae and of a sudden her mood turned as if the mention of her mother, long deceased apparently, struck an icy chord within her—a subject still raw to the touch, if I may mix my metaphors. 'You have writing in your blood then', I said in a voice intended to recover our gaiety. 'That may be', said our guest, coaxing from herself a wan smile. 'I have written a little. My

Shelley encourages me to attempt an entire book but I am not certain of a subject. Words flow from him like rays from the sun, and just as golden, only ceasing for necessary nocturnal rest; and I am not confident he fully comprehends that that is not a quality granted to all mortals in equal measure'. 'It may be', I said, 'that he knows something about you which you are not willing to believe yet. It is not unusual for us to misinterpret— or even overlook entirely—our own gifts'.

'You may be right', said Mae, her mood lightening. 'What are your gifts, beside knowing just what to say'? I was taken by surprise at her turning the subject back on me. 'I do not know that I would term it a gift, but I am quite fond of stitchwork and perhaps have a lit-tle talent for it'. As you know, my dearest, I normally do my stitching in the kitchen where the light is best but I had brought my current work to the parlour to help pass the time as we awaited our visitor (though the light in fact proved unsuitable and I took up the volume of Prior instead); nevertheless, I had the piece there beside me, beneath the sofa pillow, and I removed it to show Mae. Inexplicably I was suddenly and pro-foundly on edge, as if a schoolgirl showing my sums to a fastidious tutor—awaiting praise or persecution, either equally possible. Why I should be so desirous of this girl's approval was (is) unclear—yet another ef-fect of her magnetic persona perhaps. It was a bridal piece on which I have been working: bells and bows and baby's breath, leaving space for a date to be added, ample blues and yellows, with the thinnest thread of grey outlining the flower petals otherwise they would be lost white upon near-white.

I describe the piece in such detail to relate what enthusiasm Mae expressed over it, complimenting its harmonious balance and the precision of my sewing. 'I swear', she said, 'if I could create such beauty with needle and thread I would not bother with taking up the quill. But alas I was never encouraged in the domestic arts'. It was generous in the extreme for her to say (I am quite certain I blushed, as I am quite certain I am blushing now at recounting the praise—and I trust my darling will excuse my indulgence of vanity). My candle burns low. I had not intended to wax so while it waned, but I find that once the words begin to flow trying to cease them is tantamount to taming a raging river, the sort they have in the Americas, an Amazon or a Niagara. Perhaps it is because I feel closest to you when I am 'speaking' to you as I am now. Until tomorrow, my love—

I record a most unsettling episode. I write in the deepest recess of night, with only the last nub of a candle, and I do not wish to rummage for another, though I know precisely where Mrs O keeps them. The evening was warm so I went to bed with the window raised, against my preference as you know—although, my trepidation was less than it may have been, with Robin in the house, and also it is difficult to account but being in the company of Mrs Shelley seems to have charged me with a tiny jolt of her independent spirit. In any event we all retired somewhat early, and

I fell fast asleep. I believe I slept dreamlessly until I was suddenly awake due to a noise that was some distance off yet nevertheless quite distinct. How to describe it? It was the sound of screaming, of shrieking, but not just a single terrified voice: many. As if a massacre were being perpetrated somewhere in the district. The horrific noise struck me cold. I lay in bed fully awake, terrified, frozen. But to my own credit only for a moment or two before I thought of the children and their well-being. I robed and shod myself quickly, meanwhile the horrific sound persisted. My candle was low but I lighted it and crept into the hall, where the clamour was effectively muffled. I soon ascertained the children were secure and asleep. Robin's door was ajar however. I carefully descended the stair, feeling unsteady, which was perhaps effected by the candle's uneven flickering, on the verge of being extinguished by a persistent draft, and the partnered light and shadow which weirdly waltzed upon the papered wall of geometric design.

Just as I touched the first floor the flame went out altogether but not before I saw that the front door was open and not before I heard the terrible noise renewed. My heart pounded against its cage of ribs as if wanting escape. One might have thought that I would be paralyzed with fear, but I kept moving, possibly because the open doorway offered the only source of light, though it be just a faint twilight of contrast against the denser darkness. When I reached the threshold I saw a figure just outside, which at first started me; then the figure spoke, 'I heard a similar wailing in Reykjavik'. It was Robin, who had sensed my presence. I joined him on the walk before the house. The street was as still and as oppressive as a graveyard. Meanwhile the terrible sounds continued. 'What was it, brother'? I realised I still gripped the useless candleholder; my fingers were sore with the force I absentmindedly exerted. 'A slaughterhouse where they discovered disease among the stock. They were killing the sick animals *en bloc* to halt contagion'.

I listened to the terrified shrieks of the doomed. I imagined the damned being prodded by impish demons to a fiery hell. I had no sense of how near or how far the slaughterhouse was. As we stood there the terrible sounds dwindled to just a few animal voices, then two or three, then a single desperate lowing in the darkness. Then a silence more awful than the sound.

Robin and I returned indoors, and to our rooms. I placed what little remained of the candle on the table by my bed and relighted it, for the darkness lay heavy upon my heart.

It is the following day, *Sept 12*, bright and cheerful, and as I read over my mid-of-night missive I am tempted to remove it from this letter, to blot out what I cannot simply discard and thus excise my silliness—to have been so terrified at simply an unsettling sound. But I shall leave it intact in the hope that it shall provide you some amusement should time hang heavy and you need some pointless diversion to ward off a bout of utter boredom.

Mrs O managed to sleep through the entire episode. When I enquired regarding it this morning, as she was checking the biscuits, she was thoroughly nonplussed. Perhaps her bucolic upbringing has rendered her immune to such sounds.

I have something quite extraordinary to report. This morning, when Felix had an opportunity for unstructured reading, he brought a book from the hall and made a point of showing it to me. I did not at first grasp its significance, nor understand his zeal at brandishing it before me, holding it open. 'Read the title page, Mama', he implored. Which I did: *Queen Mab; A Philosophical Poem: With Notes*. By Percy Bysshe Shelley. Felix left me the book, implying that I may want to read it, or suggesting I should read it. I thumbed through the volume and my eyes fell upon a particular passage (it caught in my brain like a bur in the hem of my skirt):

> *When Nero*
> *High over flaming Rome with savage joy*
> *Lowered like a fiend, drank with enraptured ear*
> *The shrieks of agonising death, beheld*
> *The frightful desolation spread*

I then felt embarrassed that I had to feign recognition when Mae alluded to her husband's literary celebrity. I will need to read Mr Shelley so that I can discuss his work when Mae and I next meet. She departed with five borrowed volumes in hand but my distinct impression is that she is a supremely voracious reader. I must tear myself away for now, my love, and attend to responsibilities.

I have confessed to an obsession with writing to you, my dear, and now I find that letting go of the letter itself, of posting it to you in Dundee, requires an exercise of determination. I begin with a blank sheet but in speaking to you I seem to *create* you. It is as if I conjure you before me, and the black script which creeps across the leaf weaves you in full; the words meant for you become you. I am quite certain I should never make the admission to Rev Grayling (or perhaps to anyone). Even to me it sounds undeniably occult. Yet letting go of the letter seems very much like letting you go. Again and again. Posting them to a void, to an emptiness where they disappear forever.

My apologies, my dear; I so easily lapse into melodrama. I shall lighten the mood by informing you that Mrs O'Hair appears to have a gentleman caller. His name is Bob and he is the coalmonger's fellow. He has been delivering our coal for months, but I have noticed that he has been coming round with greater frequency enquiring as to our needs, which are a paragon of consistency and hardly warrant such surveillance. For some time he has dealt directly with Mrs O, who has a solid grasp of our culinary and caloric needs. She will speak with him in the alley, so that he need not leave horse and cart unattended. Last week I spied them through the kitchen window, and it seemed that their conversation was more animated than necessary for a common business transaction. Also, Bob had tidied his appearance. The grey hair that hung beneath his cap was a shorter length and more orderly, his beard was shaped, he was wearing a new apron, still besmudged by the unavoidable coal dust but not as tattered and worn. In addition, he sported a fresh kingsman knotted smartly at his throat. I thought little of the transformation. Then just this morning on the table in the kitchen was an assortment of dried flowers gathered with a lavender ribbon. I asked Mrs O regarding them. She became flustered, amusingly so, and was reluctant to name Bob as the source of the bouquet. I let the matter drop but found it quite charming. I know, my dear, that I must not be seen to condone such alliances; and I shall be mindful. But, still, at their ages it is difficult to see the harm—other than if I were to lose the clever Mrs O to an affair of the heart.

Mrs O, incidentally, has just delivered to me an invitation arrived by post to call on Mrs Shelley, and she has invited me to bring the children. (I fear Mrs O may have read reference to herself when she handed me the note—she came upon me so quietly, here at the table, that I did not take precaution. She may suspect I am reporting on her to her unknown master. I must assure her via my demeanor that I have not named anything unseemly.) Having only begun a new sheet, I shall have ample space to add report of our visit to the Shelley residence. There is no mention of Robin, so she must intend a sort of ladies conclave. I hope Felix shall not feel too out of place. If need be I will hand him a book, and he will be quite content.

To resume. I had thought the visit to Mrs Shelley was going to be the only interesting event of the day, but I was mistaken. Not long after I left off writing (about mid morning) Felix came to me to say there was a stranger in the alley asking after his uncle. I requested further intelligence of the fellow—I am sorry to confess that ever since my brother's arrival I have half expected the district's constabulary to come enquiring of Robin, though it is an unfounded and unfair expectation. All that our Felix was able to articulate was that the stranger had a difficult accent. I stepped into the alley. The street at the alley entrance was busy, but I found no man loitering about. I returned inside to see if I could extract anything further from Felix. Before I could commence my interrogatories, however, there was a knock at the door. Mrs O was up to her elbows in the dough she was kneading for our kidney pie, so I went to the door myself. Standing there was a tall fellow in a black coat. He had a reddish grey beard and in hand was an odd-looking cap, also black. 'Good day, madam', and he definitely bore a foreign accent, perhaps German or eastern European. 'I am enquiring to locate Robert Walton, master of the *Benjamin Franklin*'. I asked him his name, to which he proffered a card, almost as if he had been keeping it in his funny-looking cap. In handwritten script was his name and a street address. 'And your business with Captain Walton, Mr Andropov'? 'I was carpenter on the *Franklin*, Mrs Saville, and I am in possession of the captain's chest'. So this fellow, apparently a Russian, knew my name. Below his left eye began a scar that ran beneath his beard. 'Do you have the chest with you'? I enquired, glancing toward the street for a dray or cart, some sort of conveyance. 'No madam. The captain's locker is safely stowed at the room I am renting'. He nodded toward the card in my hand. I assured him that I would give my brother the message but he was not at the moment available. Mr Andropov thanked me and replaced his odd, brimless cap to his head, and by doing so I saw that the hand holding it had only the first finger and thumb, which convinced me beyond doubt he was a member of Robin's crew, a sad lot who must have experienced the extremity of hardship.

Robin was in his room. It would have been simple enough to install the Russian in the parlour and rouse my brother, who likely would be quite pleased to recover his seaman's chest. Yet I chose to send the Russian away. It was as though my brother had escaped horrible death in the plutonic land of ice, and in the person of Mr Andropov it had come calling for him— to complete what it had begun. I felt a sororal need to keep the Russian from my brother as if Mr Andropov were a personification of Death. It is an irrational idea and no doubt wholly unfair to the gentleman who must remain devoted to my brother. I resolve to be more clearheaded on the matter. I placed the card on the foyer table, where apparently my brother discovered it while I was calling upon Mrs Shelley—for Robin was absent when the children and I returned. In fact, he is absent still, which is a trifle worrisome. I remind myself he survived the Arctic waste so surely the streets of London will not be his undoing.

It is late, my dear. I am eager to share with you the visit to the Shelleys' home, but I feel I must postpone the writing until I am fresher on the morrow. Until then, my love.

Sept 13—The children are at work on their figures, and at last I can return to this letter, which should go out in this evening's post—I shall will myself to let it on its way. I must have found the visitation of the Russian more disturbing than I believed—perhaps distracted by preparing for and anticipating tea at the Shelleys' (a description soon to follow)—but I was fretful in my sleep and thus heard my brother's return in the small hours of the night, of morning really. I cannot say precisely when. He was heavyfooted which makes me suspicious that he and Mr Andropov imbibed in spirits, for Robin was rather clumsy upon the stair. He has not risen and it will be noon ere long.

It is not far to Marchmont Street. The day was overcast with grey clouds but not threatening rain, so it was a pleasant enough walk with the children to the Shelleys'. It made me think of how little I have been away from the house in recent weeks—two visits to Mr Squire's bookshop, and of course tea at Mr Smythe's but the latter hardly counts as *away* I should think. Every Sunday there is a brief pang of guilt at not taking the children to services, but then I think of little Maurice and the guilt is replaced with anger. Rev Grayling calls regularly upon us; my reception of him is always chilly, perhaps he may say *icy*. Otherwise we have had few visitors. Now, however, it seems the whole world is coming to *me*. If only you would be among the throng, my dear.

I kept the children close during our trek. Right away I noticed men noticing Agatha. She was attired most modestly, you can be assured, but there is little to be done to obscure her perfectly heart-shaped face and expressively large eyes of aquatic blue, nor the chestnut strands that fell beneath her bonnet. Beyond that there is Aggie's aura of maturity which seems to have sprung up so keenly of late. Even when she is playing dollies with Miss Buzzle it suggests a brief prelude to motherhood. I daresay she is quite a different daughter from the one you left to go on your business affair. I smile to think of your astonishment when you return.

I digress. The Shelleys' home on Marchmont Street is only trifle more than a cottage but pleasantly, though sparely, appointed. Its lack of furnishings provides the advantageous effect of airiness. The small rooms could easily become quite as claustrophobic as Mr Smythe's if Mrs Shelley is not careful. I delay myself from reporting what may be the most significant news: Mrs Shelley (Mae) has a son. As soon as we arrived she introduced the child, William, who is transitioning from mere infant to toddler. It explained why Mae included Felix and Aggie in the invitation, although the age differentials prevented true playful intercourse. Felix and Aggie went along with the boy to his nursery and entertained him with blocks and games of cat-and-rat on the chalkboard, which afforded Mae and me the opportunity to converse as adults and not merely mothers. We had only just settled with our tea when Mae surprised me by confiding that her husband was away because police informants were watching out for Mr Shelley on account of some outstanding debts—a misunderstanding that the poet was working to correct. It seemed a rather intimate confession to make to a new acquaintance, but my sense was that it has been weighing on her profoundly and she has had no one with whom to share the circumstance. I, of course, cannot relate to such pecuniary woes; however, wishing to offer some evidence of sympathy, I told of your long absence and how it affects us all. (I never forget for a moment that you are away toiling for our benefit).

There was a small writing-desk in the room—the single room that serves as both receiving room and parlour—and on it were several sheets of foolscap, along with stylus and ink. I could ascertain from my position on the sofa that there was some writing on the top sheet. 'I see you are composing—would it be your story'? Mae hesitated a moment; then, 'You are uncanny. I have scraps of ideas, of images—most have come to me in a half-waking state of dream—but they do not fit together. They will not coalesce into a lucid narrative. I am quite bewildered at the notion of writ-

ing an entire book, and think of giving it up altogether. Yet it distracts me from darker thoughts . . . darker
places'. From the nursery we heard her son William's
wet and persistent cough. I do not know from whence
the advice sprang but I offered, 'Perhaps you should
succumb to the dark thoughts, go to the dark places,
when writing I mean. Perhaps the obstacles you encounter while composing are due to your attempt to
evade them rather than embrace them'. Mae seemed
unsure how to respond. I added, 'What do I know? I
am not a writer'. 'At times', she said, 'I think I shall never be either. I feel an adventure tale may be the most
well received by a publisher; however, because of my
parents' writings, I have been thoroughly steeped in
philosophy, and I find when I compose that my mind
slips into a weightier, more metaphysical mode, wading into more turbulent topics than one normally encounters in a popular story of adventure. Thus, I am
continually stymied in my efforts'.

I did not know how to respond. Fortunately, the
conversation took a lighter turn, and we spent a pleasant pair of hours at the Shelleys' quaint home. Before
leaving Mae insisted that Felix should borrow a volume, and we were shown into her husband's study
where their books are stored in short, open-faced cases. Felix, quite excited but attempting to mask his glee,
selected a collection of Bavarian folk-stories, in German. I encouraged him to choose something in English. Mae, however, insisted it was a prudent choice:
'The young have a natural aptitude for languages. I

acquired several languages from my father's library—
to read at least. Conversing is another matter'. I noted
titles in French and Italian among the books immediately before us.

We left Mrs Shelley, and I expressed my hope that
her husband's affairs would not keep him long. While
we were visiting, the weather had turned somewhat,
and large drops rained down upon us intermittently as
we returned. It was not unpleasant but I cannot help
being anxious about the children, especially Felix,
though he appears reasonably hale. No doubt it is his
resemblance to his little brother that gives me over to
foreboding. Nevertheless, we arrived home and Mrs
O drew a warm bath for the children to light on the
side of caution. I was surprised to discover that the
washroom smelt strongly of glue, as the frugal Mrs O
had taken it upon herself to repair the bowl Aggie had
dropped. I had presumed it to be a lost cause, I must
acknowledge, so once again I was surprised by the
Irishwoman's ingenuity and industry.

This letter, I suppose, has gone on quite long
enough, my dearest. Robin has been in his room most
of the evening. I have not had opportunity to enquire
about his time with Mr Andropov and whether or
not he retrieved his chest. I suspect it may be in Maurice's room. I shall trust that my brother had the good
sense to inspect its contents before fetching it home.
I would not want any exotic vermin transported into
the house. The native sort are nuisance enough!

I shall post this letter in the morning. I trust our

placatory evening shall continue, and there shall be
nothing more to report of this eventful day.

I regret concluding this letter on such an ominous
note, but I am compelled to describe the disquieting
dream that woke me in the night. I believed I again
heard the horrific sounds of the slaughterhouse, except
much closer at hand. My fear was chiseled and cold,
like a block of ice heavy upon my heart. I wondered
if another slaughterhouse, nearer by, was the source
of the terrified and, in turn, terrifying shrieks. Then,
in the manner of dreams, I was no longer in my bed
but standing facing the room's closed door, my bare
feet on the hard and frozen floor. Amid the horrified
lowing and bleating I believed I heard a call of 'Mama'.
Again, 'Mama'. I knew it was the children. I opened the
door and stepped into the hall, which was dark save
for a wan glow coming from the stairs. Robin's door
was open but only partly and beyond the opening was
the total darkness of a tomb. The cries of 'Mama' came
from downstairs and were now so loud they split my
ears. I clasped my hands to the sides of my head to
try, in vain, to muffle the cries as I moved forward.
There was a frigid draft in the hall as if a window had
been left full open in winter. I realised my nightgown
was wet with tears I had been shedding all along. I
felt the chill of the damp material at my throat as I
began to make my way down the stairs—the light and
the children's cries increasing with every careful step. I
reached out to steady myself, uncovering my ears and
intensifying Felix's and Agatha's anguished cries for

their *Mamamamamamama*. I reached the bottom of
the steps and discovered the light was emitting from
the kitchen, and with the realisation, the very second,
the children ceased their calling out. I waded through
the terrible silence as if ice-choked floodwaters impeded my progress. I stepped into the kitchen, where
lamplight suddenly dimmed. In the sickly yellow illumination Felix and Agatha were lying on the table,
side by side and lengthwise. They turned their eyes to
me pleadingly, their little faces racked in expressions
of pain. A man stood beside the table. I reached out
and told the children to come to me; but as I said it I
saw their limbs had been severed. Their arms and legs
lay in place but lifeless upon the table. The man beside the children was the Russian, Mr Andropov. He
held his saw, its blade black with blood in the poor
light. 'I had no choice', he said in his thick accent, then
motioned with his hand that was mostly amputated
toward a small table to his left where a seaman's chest
lay open, Robin's chest presumably. I looked again
to the children and their severed arms and legs were
now the severed limbs of animals, the legs of cows and
sheep lying where their own dead limbs had lain. I
desperately attempted to make sense of the Russian's
inadequate explanation but its logic would not come
to me. A kitchen window was full open and a wintry
wind blew the chest shut, the sudden slam of its heavy
lid waking me completely. The scene vanished but the
terror of it clung to me like the dampness which had
collected on my skin.

It was a preposterous dream. Certainly Robin's old mate suggested no one so menacing. I hesitated to describe it other than in the hope that writing it out would purge the silliness from my mind (and the disquiet from my soul). Thank you for *listening*, my love.

With all

My heart,

September 14, 18—

Dear Philip,

I had hoped that a cheerful day would impart its meteorological demeanor to me, but alas we woke to steady rain which has not ceased all morning; thus my own gloom weighs upon me like a dampened cape. I think of untying the drawstring that strangles at my throat and allowing the garb to fall to the floor, unburdening me from the unwanted weight of oppressive emotions.

Once again I feel the need to apologise for laying such unwholesome intelligences at your feet. If I were you, I would want these missives to be vessels of light and good humor, rays of brilliant sunshine piercing your already bright day. It is a wonder you open them at all as they must land like casts of lead in your box . . . in your life. Perhaps I would be less inclined to fill these letters with such dreary thoughts if I had someone with whom to share them in person. I long to speak with Robin about his adventures in the snow-

fields of the north—it must have been harrowing in
the extreme—but he has been little more than a spec-
tre in the house: coming and going, rising and retiring
at odd hours, and, most trying of all, being as commu-
nicative as a shroud-wrapped mummy. I know I must
not rush him; he will tell what he will when he is ready.
I believe I am anxious in part because if Robin were
to unfold the narrative of his far-northern adventure
and its hardships, he would afford me the opportunity to share some of my cares in turn, tit for tat. It is
so difficult to appreciate something in the moment:
appreciation is so often a product of retrospection. I
have come to realize how much I miss the earliest days
of our marriage, those nearly two years before Agatha
arrived. You were of course busy with your work,
needing to establish yourself, yet we managed to find
hours to talk, to truly communicate, soul to soul—not
that every subject was deadly serious: we would often
make each other laugh—but no matter how light or
how leaden the discourse we shared a perfect understanding of honesty, of communion without pretense,
without barriers. The months awaiting Aggie's arrival,
when I was terrified at the prospect of childbirth, our
ability to talk, my opportunity to share with you my
manifold trepidations, helped me to manage the terror, to prevent it from driving me mad with irrational
and overpowering fears.

Then Agatha was here, pink and peevish and profoundly needful; and everything changed, especially
between you and me. Even amid the chaos and mar-

row-deep exhaustion I noticed the change, felt your keen absence even though you came and went as usual. However, our time together to talk, to truly sympathize, spirit to spirit, that had disappeared. I recognised the fact, noted the disappearance, but what I did not comprehend was that that intimacy was vanished forever, as if burgled by clever thieves who snatch their precious object then slip stealthily back into the blackest hour of night.

Perhaps these letters and my compulsive writing of them are an attempt to retrieve it, to resurrect it at last. Forgive me my writing them, my love; you do not know how I have missed you and for how long.

I fear I have written myself into quite the blue mood, indigo even—and you as well! I must attempt to rectify the matter. I must concentrate on the positive. For example, the glorious smell of scones that fills the house thanks to Mrs O's baking. She has mixed a touch of cinnamon with the batter, so the homely scent is tinged with that festive spice. Agatha of course assisted with the recipe, while Felix, the old soul, sat in the corner reading, or perhaps more often than not glancing through the rain-streaked window at the colourless day beyond. No doubt the language difficulties of the German folk-stories, borrowed from Mr Shelley's study, impeded Felix's reading enjoyment and encouraged introspection via gazing at the inclement weather.

The wet conditions outdoors have also coaxed the wonderfully musty smell of old books to rise indoors, which nicely complements Mrs O's baking sweets. Warmth from the kitchen radiates throughout the rooms—if not in *fact*, at least in *belief*—which also adds a pleasantness to this grey day.

'So you see', I tell myself, 'your moroseness is quite ill-founded and must be quitted at once'. This shall be my badge going forward, my dear. Perhaps I shall commit it to stitches and hang the piece where I shall view it every day.

As if on cue, the moment I completed the previous sentence there was a caller at the door. Who in the world? I thought—on this rainy day? Mrs O admitted Reverend Grayling and showed him into the parlour. I heard his voice from my place in the kitchen. I was surprised at the specific timing of his visit but not, in general, that he had come. He has been a regular caller in your absence, under the pretense of checking on this fatherless family while you are away, but his purpose is more to do with leading this stray sheep back to the fold. Rev Grayling was standing staring out the rain-obscured window when I joined him. The shoulders of his coat were a darker black with water— his hat and his top-coat were dripping on the stand in the foyer. He turned and greeted me, gazing down the edge of his beaked nose. He is still tall in spite of his stooped posture. I invited him to sit and we occu- pied the adjacent chair and sofa. Mrs O was preparing fresh tea, I informed him (hoping, to be honest, he would say he would not be staying long enough for tea—he made no such proclamation). I do not wish

to be uncharitable to the Reverend but his presence in
the house brings back with painful vividness the experience of Maurice's death (tears come to my eyes even
at the writing of it). The betrayal of his illness, the futility of prayer, the salt-laced inadequacy of comfort.

Rev G began with niceties of polite conversation
then quickly came to the point of his visit, which I believed I knew. However, he surprised me by querying
in regard to my brother. 'I hear that Master Robert is
returned from sea'. I hesitated before offering affir-
mation, though I am not certain why. I suppose I expected Rev G to note the miraculous nature of Robin's
return and attempt to offer it, rhetorically, as a kind
of counterweight to *God's calling little Maurice home*
(was that not how he phrased it at the service, again
and again, *ad nauseam*?). I was prepared for this turn
of logic; it has been a syllogism of my own since Robin's arrival—one whose solution I reject as false, as ab-
surd even.

I was not prepared, however, for the Reverend to
say, 'Is your brother quite well? There are those with
concerns'. 'What sort of concerns'? 'Master Robert's
behavior has been seen as . . . erratic by some'. 'Erratic? How so'? I said, but I knew how, or believe I did—
erratic in the ways he has been here, under our roof.
Observed by those who do not know him, who do not
know what he has endured, what he has sacrificed—I
could imagine the cause of their concerns. Nevertheless I felt a surge of protectiveness toward my little
brother. 'Who is the accuser'? Rev G shifted his bulk

uneasily in his chair. 'No one is making accusations—
there are those who are worried. Good Christians
who have expressed their concerns'. It just slipped out
in my pique: 'Yes, well, the Church has a long history
of good Christians expressing their concerns, does it
not? Their concerns regarding heresy, their concerns
regarding others' sins'.

He placed his hands on his knees and thus exaggerated his stooped posture. His knuckles were red
and raw from the cold. 'Mrs Saville . . . Margaret', he
said more mildly, 'it is not like that at all.' He became
more erect. 'There are reports that Robert has been
seen having animated conversations with absent interlocutors'. 'So he has muttered to himself in public;
that is hardly a crime against the good citizens of London'. 'Not muttering to himself. Actual conversation
but with someone who was not present. A phantom
if you will'. 'My brother has had some spirits since his
return—who can blame him'? 'He was not inebriated,
Margaret; he was quite sober, as it was reported'. 'My
word, your reporters are impressively thorough. They
should be in the employ of the Privy Council'. 'There is
more: Robert seems unusually alert and watchful, as if
expecting to be set upon at any moment'. 'My brother
has been through a great ordeal; I should think it quite
natural for him to still be in the mode of survivalist.
That should withdraw over time'.

Perhaps Rev Grayling sensed the futility of further
discourse given the state into which his visit had delivered me. Shortly he gathered his coat and hat and

returned to the grey, wet world, but not before re-
marking that I should call upon him should I need
anything—implying, I think, that I may need assistance with Robin. Mrs O was just bringing the tea as
he was effecting his exit. I had Mrs O place the tray
on the table, and I poured myself a cup. I had difficulty concentrating and I needed a quiet moment. I
sat for a long while, cup and saucer in hand, contemplating Rev Grayling's visit. After a time I was able to
acknowledge that its most troubling aspect was my
sense that the Reverend was in the right—to a degree
at least: Robin's behaviour was cause for concern.

I am not retracting my earlier judgement that Robin is harmless toward the children and me. Not at all,
my dear! But I have been worried, I realized, that Robin may be harmful to himself. I did not want to believe
it so I did not dare utter it, even internally, not fully
anyway. It was a thought which loitered about a dark
corner of my mind, and I had been doing all that I
could to prevent its stepping into the light; or, as if a
player in the wings, now in full view of the anticipating audience.

In some ways it was a relief to acknowledge the
thought, if only to myself. However, the relief of that
idea instantly surrendered to a disquieting one: Who
were Rev Grayling's informants? I recalled the agents
who Mrs Shelley said watched her home to apprehend
her debt-burdened husband, or at least to apprehend a
clue regarding his whereabouts. Could similar agents
be spying on our home? Taking note of Robin's com-

ings and goings? Watching the children as they play in the alley? Recording my visits to Mr Smythe and Mrs Shelley?

Of course not. It was a nonsensical notion, born of my disturbing dialogue with old Rev Grayling.

As exasperating and unsettling as his line of enquiry was, after a time I discovered that beneath my irritation was a current of relief that he had not broached the subject of my truancy from services. There is a piece of me, buried well deep, which feels a spasm of guilt at not taking the children to church, a product of my own upbringing planted by my father and watered and fertilized by the Church itself; but instantly I recalled the charade of it all: of a benevolent, paternalistic God who watches over His flock, especially His little children, and Whose stern guidance helps us to avoid falling into the Pit of Eternal Flames. He certainly did not bestow His benevolence upon our Maurice; nor for that matter, it seems, half the children of London; nor their shattered, bereaved parents left to carry on in their little ones' constant and conspicuous absence.

I am sorry, my dear—I know . . . I know . . . I must not go on with this bitter and spiteful blasphemy. But where may I give voice to it other than here, in these private pages intended only for my husband, who already knows the wounded mind and shattered heart of his wife? For surely we *know* that at which we can easily *guess*, as one knows the forever sun blazes in the heavens even when it is fully obscured behind a dense curtain of clouds (as it is today). Its light filters through, diffused and dulled but evidence of the star's distant ferocity nonetheless.

Listen to me, waxing philosophic, poetic even. Perhaps it is the influence of Mr Shelley's book, which I had some opportunity to peruse prior to Rev Grayling's visit. The poet's voice and words, in all their eloquent impact, give mine agency, a permission of sorts to flower forth. Bold and embittered.

No doubt I have flowered forth quite enough—a veritable jungle of philosophic flora—and I shall cease, especially since I must see to the children and the progress of their lessons. Due to Felix's infatuation with the book of German folk-tales, for his geography lesson I charged him with trying his hand at map-making by drawing a likeness of Deutschland. One of Uncle's books has a map of central Europe as its end-papers. Though probably somewhat out-of-date, it served reasonably well as Felix's model. I shall report as to the success (or not) of his cartographical efforts.

Sept 15—I woke this morning realizing that the thought of Rev Grayling's informants had been weighing upon my mind. Also: Where had Robin been on his rambles that he should encounter those who report to the Reverend? For the past twenty-four hours he has been keeping to his little room like a monk to his cell. Mrs O delivered him tea twice yesterday, without his requesting it, or for that matter sharing any sort of word with any of this house's inhabitants. She

said both times he was lying abed, though her sense
was that he was not sleeping. When she took him the
second pot of tea, the first was empty, so at least he
took some nourishment. The same was true of his other teapot when she retrieved it this morning, she said.
At that time Robin did appear fast asleep. No doubt
his body needs an excess of repose to fully recover.
His body and his spirit. Mrs O is determined that he
should consume something more than tea, however.
She took him up a bit of boiled brisket from yesterday's supper and a poached egg, along with a pair of
biscuits with her currant jam.

As I have been writing, my dear, the morning post
arrived and there is a letter for Robin from the Russian, Mr Andropov (his hand is distinct—you know
what I mean). I can only imagine that it is an invitation
to accompany him on another excursion in the city. It
occurs to me that perhaps the most expedient way to
discover Rev Grayling's informants would be to follow
Robin and Mr A to see who may be spying *them*. Even
as I write these words I know the foolishness of the
proposal—yet I find the idea of it intriguing. To be at
once out in the world and yet also apart from it—at
least as far as Robin would be concerned. In his mind
his sister would be safely stowed at home (working at
her stitches or tending to the children or, most likely,
writing a letter to her husband!) but at the same time I
would be occupying his world, at least the edges of it:
one must not be too close if one hopes to observe the
observers, that is, Rev G's 'good Christians', his eyes

and ears.

I shall make preparations by placing my wrap and hat and shoes in the washroom, where they will be unnoticed but quickly accessible whenever Robin departs for his appointment with Mr A. I must acknowledge that I feel the exhilaration of adventure, the thrill of subterfuge, yet also the guilt of deception and the naggings of common sense. Nevertheless I am resolved to follow Robin when he exits the house. I shall leave off for now to put my plan into place.

Several hours have passed. Where to begin? Robin descended from his room about midday and read the note from his Russian mate; it must have been as I surmised for a bit later, at about four o'clock, Robin ventured out to meet Mr Andropov—or so I presumed, for he did not say a word regarding it. Rather, he ate then returned to his room to read. He considered taking his book to the alley, but the weather was not conducive to outdoor reading: not raining per se but there is a distinct nip in the air, a coolness that is deceptively penetrating. I wondered that the wrap I secreted away in the washroom would be adequate. I lingered in the kitchen throughout the afternoon, waiting and wondering if in fact Robin would leave the house—until finally he came downstairs and left via the front door, still without a word. I stepped into the washroom, dressed with haste, then entered the alley. I said nothing to Mrs O, who was resting in her room off the kitchen; nor the children, who were contentedly engaged in the parlour.

I knew in which direction Robin would turn on the street if he were going to Mr A's boardinghouse, which is in a neighbourhood of some dubious establishments where he may have been rendezvousing with his friend. When I first entered the street, rushing but not running, I did not see Robin (and I half hoped I had lost him already so that I could abandon the plan of which I had already grown wary). Soon, however, I picked up his trail, spying him before the tobacconist's just before turning onto Taviton. The streets were of course bustling, which made it more difficult to keep track of Robin but at the same time it helped to obscure me, a solitary woman on the walk. Our district seems filled with such women—poor widows, perhaps, scraping by, and women with families who must labor to provide roof and table for their children. I count myself fortunate, my dear, to be among them only in the spirit-stifling street and not in sorrowful circumstance. I had distracted myself and nearly forgotten my primary object: to spy those who are spying my brother. To do so I was required to retreat to a position which made it exceedingly difficult to keep Robin in view. However, there was no remedy for the conundrum; I fell back. (Is that not the term generals use to describe the battlefield maneuver? Perhaps I shall ask Mr Smythe.) Fortunately Robin did not appear to be of a mind to make haste, gazing from time to time in shop windows and generally effecting the pace of one out for a leisurely stroll. Even still, I would lose sight of him in the busy thoroughfare, especially

at cross streets, and at times believe I had lost him altogether. Then I would catch a glimpse at this window
or that, or once pausing to listen to a beggar street mu-
sician sawing at a dilapidated viola.

My watching was of course complicated by my also
watching for those who may be watching Robin. There
was no shortage of candidates. I tried to think what
Rev Grayling's good Christians would look like on the
streets. I could not form a definite picture. They may
be man or woman, old or young—a child even, only
Agatha's age, but a boy, an acolyte on Rev G's altar. I
imagined the Reverand's congregants, convinced as I
was that his informants were members of his church—
though likely as it was, it was still only surmise.

Suddenly a new thought came to me: What if I cannot observe the observers because they are already
observing me observing Robin? My imagination then
fired a new tableau, and I saw myself walking along
the busy street: A woman of medium height, narrow
of shoulder but perhaps that defect is somewhat hid-
den beneath the woolen wrap; brown hair gathered in
a bun beneath her bonnet but with some stray strands
falling down (I could feel them against my neck);
long-fingered hands at the ends of my dress-sleeves,
cadaverously pale save for the stains of ink, the dark
marks of these compulsively written epistles; and a
face whose narrowness complements her shoulders—
but what its expression? Probably a trace of worry just
now, in the set of the jaw and a gathering of horizontal
lines at the eyes; yet also a spark of determination de-

rived from a protective instinct; and I would hope an overall intelligence, largely communicated via the eyes and brow, sea green and wide set, respectively. And should her bonnet blow off in a blustery breeze, an all but impossible occurrence due to its black ribbon being tied in a bow beneath her chin, one may note the early grey at the temples, like hoarfrost selectively formed, or (better) ash fired by fret and clinging fast.

Yet there was nothing to be done about the observational situation—other than to keep Robin in view and hope that in some way I may discover those surveilling him. The streets were darkening, and I had no wish to be out, an unescorted woman, at full night. Besides, it would become increasingly difficult to maintain my brother's track, even with the efforts of the lantern-lighters. Fortunately Robin had not taken such a circuitous path that I had lost my orientation. I knew precisely where I was and how to return home. Robin paused at the cart of a vendor who was selling some sort of broiled and heavily spiced meat, mutton perhaps. Robin purchased some of the meat in brown paper, conically formed; then continued his amble, eating with his fingers as he walked. The outing had stoked my appetite and I did have a few pennies in the pocket of my dress, but I found the smell of the greasy and exotically spiced mutton rather nauseating. I nodded to the black-bearded, swarthy-skinned vendor as I passed by his aromatic cart.

Robin turned into a narrow street that was of a decidedly darker character. I hesitated to follow; how-

ever, there was no visible danger—only silly womanly
fears—so I stayed the course. Before I could enter, a
pair of fellows hurried into the ancient street ahead
of me. There was something about their tempo and
intensity that suggested they may be following my
brother. Even as I drew the conclusion I knew it may
just be the result of my overly energetic imagination.
But whether genuine or fanciful, my belief about their
intent spurred me onward regardless of the street's
shabbiness. The differences between Taviton and
Harrow Street were abundantly clear, especially in regard to the latter's squalidness. The sheer population
marked it as a street of especial meanness—it seemed
thousands had been lodged in a space meant for just a
fraction of that number. And every age was represented out of doors, from infants to the elderly, and each
exuded its unique brand of want and woe, from the
wailing of babes to the cursing of the mature and the
moaning of the agedly infirm. The facades of the squat
buildings were near black with grime, and boards or
tattered blankets covered the majority of the windows,
the panes of glass shattered, no doubt, through a long
history of hostile domestic frays.

Seeing all the various manifestations of want it
came to me that maybe the fellows following Robin
were not agents of Rev Grayling (now, suddenly, it
seemed a ridiculous premise), but rather ruffians who
may believe Robin a somewhat prosperous person. He
was, after all, attired in your older garments, cleverly
seamstressed by Mrs O'Hair; thus he was costumed

as a gentleman in comparison to the throngs on the
street, this street in particular. (I know that it must be
worrisome to think of me there as well, but I obviously came to no harm as I am telling the tale—the
curse of the first-person narrator, if this were a mere
story spun to amuse of a winter's evening.) One of the
fellows following Robin, as I interpreted their intention, wore a coat of vivid green, worn, patched and
soiled but still an unusual hue in this dun-tinted district. As such, I was able to keep track of him more
easily, while Robin himself was fully obscured among
the unwashed multitude. People were bumping into
me, or I was bumping into them; indeed, there were
so many milling pedestrians, like cattle in a crowded market, it was difficult to say which. Throughout, I
kept a sharp eye on the green coat. Hence I was fully
aware when the vividly appareled fellow and his more
somberly dressed companion disappeared between
dilapidating buildings down a narrow alley, lined, I
soon discovered, with all manner of cast aside crates
and other less wholesome refuse.

I faced a dilemma. I could not say with certainty
that Robin had entered this alley. Pausing, I strained to
see farther along the street, in hopes I may spy Robin
and therefore have been mistaken about the objective
of the fellow in green and his mate. But I spied nothing of my brother, which may have meant he in fact
turned into this filthy alley, or I had simply lost sight
of him in the street and perhaps even then he was sitting down to a drink with Mr Andropov. How stupid

and pointless it would be to be murdered or worse in this fetid alley if Robin were, in truth, nowhere about. That was my thinking as I proceeded forward, leaving behind the commotion and relative safety of Harrow Street. (Perhaps there is a trickle in my blood of whatever runs rampantly through my brother's veins that thrusts him into places foreign and perils unknown.) Immediately my eye found the green coat, standing apart like a garden oasis, an Eden in fact, amidst a region devastated by countless calamities: fire and famine, pestilence and plague, destitution and draught.

The alley was narrow and not altogether straight, thus with the debris and its higgledy-piggledy course, I could not see what was before me more than a few yards, and even then it was consistently obfuscated by piles of wretched refuse. Therefore I only glimpsed the verdant coat two or three times before the melee began. It started with a dog barking, some sort of medium breed of hound perhaps, quite adamant in its protestations. Then there was human shouting—for want of a better word. I would perhaps write 'screaming' but I feel *scream* has a feminine connotation and these were definitely male vocalizations. I had quite frozen in my path, listening with my own sort of canine ferocity. Only for a moment or two, however, for it was interrupted by boisterous movement back toward my position. By instinct I stepped behind some festering crates and knelt near as I was able to the filthy wall. I was now quite convinced that these fellows had nothing to do whatsoever with Rev Grayling but were rather a pair of ne'er-do-wells or even cut-throats who were of a mind to fall upon my unsuspecting brother for their own malignant purpose.

My musings were halted when the men ran past me in their haste to exit the alley. The somber-suited fellow knocked over a crate which was, I hoped, shielding me from view. It was no matter because their only aim was to reach the alley's entrance and the relative calm of the street. I noted that the green-coated man was heavily bearded, and a wild mane of coal-black hair flowed from his battered coachman's hat. His companion, by comparison, was that most ironic of adjectives: nondescript, almost to the point of disappearing from one's field of vision. The dog had ceased its bellowing and once the pair had passed, all was weirdly quiet. My sisterly devotion returned with the end of the immediate danger, and I wondered at Robin's well-being. Still kneeling at the alley's brick wall I listened acutely. I detected the clicking scurry of vermin somewhere nearby, and there were the street sounds, more muffled than they ought to have been by the distance but the alley's clutter also cut the noise, which was becoming the noises of night in the city.

Perhaps I possess a more intrepid soul than I give myself credit, or perhaps it was due to the strength of my sororal instinct—but whichever the case I rose from my semi-exposed position near the brick wall and proceeded deeper into the bowel of the gloomy alley. I moved forward slowly and, yes, charily; but, indeed, forward. I therefore had ample time to consider

my course. You will think me silly, my dear, or perhaps even touched when I say that I thought of Ulyss-
es' descent to the underworld. I recalled the sacrificial
blood he spilled to call forth the shades, and for the
briefest of moments I believed I saw just such a mark
at my feet in the alley: a dark patch of blood. It was in
fact some other, equally loathsome fluid that lay in a
puddle upon the grimy ground.

To conclude, I discovered no one else in the alley,
not my brother nor even the dog I had heard—though
my frayed imagination conjured a sort of presence:
a feeling I was not alone, that there were eyes upon
my back no matter which way I turned. I wondered
that maybe some shades had been summoned after
all. I had the unaccountable notion that it was you,
my dear, who watched me and that I would turn and
find you there. I turned and turned, and was disap-
pointed each revealing revolution. There were several
doors scattered along the alley, and I conjectured that
Robin, the dog, and whoever else the pair of ne'er-do-
wells may have encountered had already absconded
indoors somewhere. Satisfied that at least I did not
find my brother mortally injured in some wretched
corner, I removed myself from the 'underworld' and
returned home without further incident. Once on the
street, among clearly corporeal beings, I no longer felt
the ghostly presence at my heel. I do not know that
Mrs O or the children missed me at all.

I must conclude this tome, my love, and I shall do so
with the assurance that I am quite well and that I will

exercise more sense from now onward. I realize that as wife and mother I have a duty to the children; and it is selfish to risk my safety except in the sole charge of protecting and preserving them (I write this so that you do not have to trouble).

Your

Devoted

Wife, *M*

Dear Philip,

I shall begin with the 'news' that Mrs Shelley is intending to call this afternoon, and I have in turn invited Mr Smythe. I seem to forget the kindly gentleman until I desire something of him; and I detest that quality in others. Mrs O was quite in favor of the idea of my entertaining, and she suggested making a pastry which she calls 'the bishop's buttons'. I believe Mrs O has been stimulated by the break in the monotony of our daily schedule, which had been a paragon of consistency since her arrival. I had not thought of the possibility of her suffering under the slow but steady weight of routine, as the Church used to crush its hostile witnesses by the addition of one small stone upon another, until either confession or expiration, whichever came first to the supine recipient. After my outing, foolish and selfish though it was, I can understand the desire for stimulation beyond the humdrum everyday. At the same mo-

ment I recognize the luxury of boredom, as searching
for food, for shelter, for *safety* would certainly be stim-
ulating departures from the daily dullness of eating,
sleeping, and failing to fall victim to foul play—and I
certainly appreciate your efforts to prevent those sorts
of exhilarating experiences. (I can envisage your shaking your head at my silliness to register complaint on
the grounds of consistent comforts.)

I assume Mae will bring her darling little boy, William, named for his maternal grandfather; thus Agatha and Felix will have a charge for the duration of
the visit. I can imagine that Mae is lonely for her poet
husband, as he manoeuvres to elude the deputies who
wish to jail him for debt which he is simultaneously
attempting to discharge. It seems a profound logical
fallacy (that is to say, perfectly *il*logical) to lock up
someone who owes money, thus making it more difficult to secure the needed funds. I suppose the strategy
is to extract means the debtor may be attempting to
conceal—or to force family and friends to intercede
on the imprisoned one's behalf. It must bear fruit in
most cases; otherwise the authorities would cease the
practice. Meanwhile wives and children bear the burden of their absent husband and father.

My apologies for sliding into that tangent, my dear.
No doubt my own history (with Papa's death and my
family's subsequent collapse, financial and otherwise)
has left me especially sympathetic to Mrs Shelley's situation. Hopefully I can provide a few hours of congenial distraction from her cares.

I have never been inclined toward daytime napping, as you know, but I must admit to feeling uncommonly fagged, and the idea of such repose is attractive at the moment. It is as if yesterday's exhilaration must be mirrored by an equal depletion of energy—a scientific law of some sort. I perhaps have a better understanding of Robin's inclination to sequester himself in Maurice's room hour upon hour. He must have suffered a very grave depletion of energy during his travails in the far north—physical energy, yes, of course, but even more so a kind of spiritual energy: an energy of the soul, of the psyche. I worry that, unlike physical exhaustion, simple rest will not be adequate to restoring Robin's psychic energy. Yet I find the question of what would be adequate unanswerable. This windy diatribe on the subject of depleted energy has only emphasized my need for rest. I shall continue, my love, after Mrs Shelley's and Mr Smythe's visit.

The rest was a mistake it seems. Of course I must pass little Maurice's door on way to our room. I have never told you but I am inclined to reach out and touch the ancient maple of the door as I pass—I suppose emblematic of a mother's wish to touch once more the dear face of a departed child, though the gesture only brings back a momentary stab of grief, an instant's recollection of the loss. Today was no different. Behind the door I heard Robin's quiet movements, too quiet to even begin to guess at his activity. Yet the sound of his presence may have exaggerated the piercing stab of grief, for the moment I lay in bed a most vivid recollection commenced. I hesitate to term it a 'dream' as it was far more potent than an unbidden fantasy—also it was nearly pure memory with none of the mind's faculty for embellishment. It was the recollection of an event that I have not shared with you, nor any living soul. After Maurice finally succumbed to the pneumonia which his frail little frame had fought so courageously, and I was struck with grief so severe I felt as though I too was drowning—or, worse, buried alive with the terrible weight of the grave's dirt pressing, pressing, pressing upon me, slowly suffocating me. On the doctor's advice, you administered to me a strong draught of brandy and bade me sleep, which I had not done for days due to my vigil at Maurice's bedside. I did sleep for a time but awoke to a silent house. Even though I knew the vision may finish me, may complete my death which began with our little boy's final, labored breath, I summoned the strength to rise from bed. Too exhausted to bother with robe and slippers, I softly strode the cold hall in only my sleeping gown, whose ghostly form seemed to me like a shroud in my tortured imagining. I went to Maurice's room, and slowly pushed back the door, the ancient hinges of which wept at our devastating loss. Maurice's tiny frame lay covered on his bed, just as he had lain in life, struggling to keep hold of it, only a few hours before—though I knew not how long. In my shattered state, grief-stricken and exhausted, I had lost all account of time. A wan light entered through the window, casting a sickly illumination on Maurice's lifeless form, but I knew not if it were the pale light of dawn or of dusk. The window sash was drawn up to allow an airing of the room in spite of the chill night (or day)—as if one might draw death and devastation from the room as one does an unpleasant odor. I took an unsteady step toward our little boy and his name was upon my trembling lips—when the sheet that covered him fluttered as if a hand had moved—and again. Perhaps he was not dead after all; such mistakes have been made; doctors are hardly infallible in spite of all their airs. I rushed to Maurice and pulled back the covering. I searched his pallid body for another sign of life. I put my hands upon his cold face and beseeched him to move again. 'Mama is here, Mama is here. Awake, little dove . . . awake', I pleaded. But there was only the bloodless hue and immobile limbs. His lids were not fully closed and beneath them I saw the lusterless orbs of the dead. Just then I felt the icy draft upon my fingers, some chill breeze blown in from the open window, and I understood that the fluttering sheet had been only that: a cruel hoax, God's having the last laugh.

I believed I was depleted of tears but a few final drops fell on Maurice's withered face. I wiped them away before replacing the cover exactly as it had been, and I returned to my bed, my desolation renewed and finally complete; I doubted that I would awaken . . . for how could my fractured heart, shattered into a thousand shards, continue beating? Why would it wish to?

I have never shared this story with you. When I

awoke, with full light at our window, the visitation to Maurice's room seemed patently unreal, replete with the residue of a terrible, terrible dream. Now it has returned as a dream which like memory confirms the reality of the event. I used to feel that Maurice's spirit lingered in the house, in his room especially. That is why I was reluctant to separate Agatha and Felix by replacing one of them to Maurice's vacant room—though my own rationale was not clear to me. If something of Maurice remained, I did not want him feeling unwelcome . . . on account of his merely being deceased. (I know how it sounds, especially now that I have articulated it.) Nor did I want Aggie or Felix infected by Maurice's death—not the disease which ravaged his lungs, mind you: rather, I thought of death as a condition into which they could be persuaded—just as the devil was seen to lure the young into his ranks, to write their names in his black book. Vaguely I imagined Death attracting them from the realm of the living to his own cold and colourless realm.

It is true that when Robin arrived I had little choice but to put him in Maurice's unused room. Beyond that, however, my concerns did not apply to my brother. He had already visited the icy region of the dead and had managed to return, if not in whole at least in part. Of course I was not thinking so lucidly at the time. Only in retrospect can I sort through my thoughts and feelings, can I begin to make some sense of them (though I suspect there is meagre sense to be made). I have gone on so, I barely have time to prepare for my guests.

For this visit, Mae was a paragon of punctuality. A hired girl had transported William, carrying him in a sling around her neck. Poor thing, she was thoroughly fatigued when they arrived. Mae dismissed the girl, who I think was barely older than Agatha, with the instruction to return in two hours' time. However, I insisted the girl stay and keep Mrs O company, thus affording her the opportunity to take some refreshment. That decided, we convened the visit in the parlour. Mae has the fairest complexion, and the exertion of walking had added paint-strokes of pink which stood out especially in the context of her dress's indigo dye. I noted that William had inherited the characteristic from his mother, as his thin cheeks were quite flushed. Shortly his coughing commenced, and I began to fret that the scarlet patina was more ominous than a simple epidermal trait. Felix was entertaining the boy with some of his old blocks. I instructed Felix to return to his lessons; he began to protest that they were complete but he recognized his mother's tone and exited the parlour, no doubt to find his book. Leaving the child was not a sacrifice. Mrs O had brought us tea, and perhaps the perceptive Irishwoman was of a similar mind: Shortly after I sent Felix away, Mrs O asked if 'Miss Aggie might n't lend a hand in the kitchen'. Little William sat on the rug between his mother's feet and manipulated the wooden blocks for his amusement. He seemed to be trying to make words or pieces of words—harbinger of a prodigy, which would not be surprising given his parentage.

After Mae had had some tea and we had dispensed with the usual pleasantries, she enquired as to whether Captain Walton were at home. Hearing him called that, though perfectly appropriate, threw me a bit off-center for a moment. Perhaps his entitled nomenclature spoken aloud made real certain aspects of his voyage which had remained in the region of abstraction in spite of my knowing their veracity and validity. After all, one could not look upon poor Robin without accepting as fact that he was the survivor of hardship—and only just. Still, it seems odd, even to me, that such a simple utterance could affect so completely one's perception of the material world; and I wonder if it was not so much the phrase itself—'Captain Walton'—as the way Mae had said it: her voice and intonation dressing the words in authority. I could imagine Robin's men pronouncing their master's name in just that manner as they looked to him for guidance, for strength, for resolve in their bleakest moments—the name carrying their dependency on him to lead them out from the baneful bergs of ice into open water and an unencumbered path to their homeport. And he did; Captain Walton did.

These impressions, or the faintest framework of them, passed through my mind in that unsettled moment before I responded to Mae's enquiry that Robin was at home but most likely engaged at present—though in truth I have little idea what Robin is engaged in during the long hours he remains in his room—other than, it seemed, sleep.

'Why do you ask'? I enquired. Mae hesitated before reaching into the bag she had brought with her. I imagined it held items for little William; and no doubt that is true too. At present, however, she removed some papers, folded in half and bound with a black ribbon. She held the small parcel in her lap as she spoke: 'I have informed you that I am engaged in writing something. I believe it is more accurate to say I am engaged in struggling to write something. I feel that my subject draws nearer yet is still out of view. When I met you and your brother at Mr Smythe's, it struck me as a sign of some sort. I spent time in Scotland a number of years ago and while there I conceived of a yarn about a captain and crew who explore the Polar region. I heard of sailors with such ambitions from the mariners who counted Dundee as their homeport. I wrote the beginning of a narrative about just such an explorer. I have copied it out here'—she indicated the papers in her pale hands—'and I was hoping that Captain Walton may be so kind as to read the embryonic tale and share his unadorned opinion, especially in regards to its air of authenticity. I did not think this would be my subject matter—in fact, it seems rather far from it—but the chance encounter . . . well, it is not wise to challenge one's Muse when she finally begins to whisper in one's ear, is it'?

She proffered the small bundle. In truth I am dubious as to the wisdom of Robin's poring over Mae's narrative. He seems reluctant to take up the pen on his own behalf—he has yet to comment on the literary projects described by Mr Havens, of the Geographic Society, whose card rests in the drawer of the foyer table. Nevertheless, I accepted Mae's offering and assured her I would share the pages with Robin.

She also took from her bag two of the volumes I had lent her, and we were just beginning to discuss her reaction when Mrs O interrupted our conversation, begging our pardons, to report that Mr Smythe was at the alley door, and for some reason could not come inside—when she is speaking rapidly I struggle with her brogue. I excused myself from Mae's company and proceeded directly through the hall and kitchen to the door. Opening it, I found Mr S and a boy of approximately Aggie's age who was clearly an urchin of the streets. 'I was en route to responding to your kind invitation, madam, when I spied this fellow loitering about, peeping in your windows'. Mr S, dressed again in his regimental reds, had a hand upon the boy's shoulder. 'He claims to have a message for you'. My heart began to beat against my breast. 'For me'? I said, somewhat breathless. 'Yes, mum'. He reached a hand black with dirt and coal char into a torn pocket and produced a folded slip of paper. I had no patience for delay and unfolded the message there in the alley, thinking it must be from you, my dear, and wondering why you had not sent it by regular post, feeling in the instant it was a bad omen—all this while unfolding the single sheet of paper, which read,

Unable to meet – agents watching everywhere. S

The reference to watchful agents, ubiquitous ones at that, prompted me to think of Rev Grayling and his many spies. I must say my skills to comprehend the message were diminished by the disappointment at realizing the note had not been sent by you. The single 'S' for a signature confounded me. I was about to inform the messenger he had the wrong address and send him on his way: Then the context of the abbreviated missive came to me. 'For whom are you looking'? I enquired. 'For you, mum. For Mrs Shelley'. 'You have missed your mark, but I shall put it into her hand'. The boy fingered his ragged cap and attempted to run off, but Mr S still had hold of him. He loosened his grip and generously gave the boy a sixpence for his trouble. I led our neighbour to the parlour directly and settled him in a chair with a cup of tea as I delivered the note to its intended recipient. She explained what was already obvious. She and Shelley planned through intermediaries to meet here, hoping the clandestine reunion would be missed by the deputies who were intent on jailing her husband. Though she did not say as much, I received the impression that the secret rendezvous was Mae's primary reason for visiting.

For an instant I felt a prick of pique, a twinge of temper at the perceived deception, but I soon realised that I would quickly stoop to an innocent charade if it meant meeting you, my dear. I can forgive a lonely heart much.

The three of us commenced a congenial conversation. Still, I had difficulty relaxing, listening to little William with his wet cough. It was too reminiscent of Maurice when he first became ill, before we knew (accepted?) the seriousness of his condition.

Dr Higgins insisted that the compresses, if properly applied with rigorous precision, would heal his sick lungs, their potent and pungent aromatic vapors would loosen the corruption and free his lungs to breathe. For the longest time the doctor maintained that Maurice's coughing was a positive sign, that the compresses were working. Even after Maurice began coughing blood, the doctor was emphatic that the treatments be maintained. I believed him. I *wanted* to trust in his practice. I could not accept that our little dove was slipping away, even though children die every day. Our little boy could not; must not. Meanwhile Rev Grayling visited us more and more often; and more and more I thought of him as the Angel of Death. With the same level of insistence as Dr Higgins, Rev Grayling insisted upon ministering to Maurice, but I knew, even from the commencement of his visits, they were not the ministrations of healing—they were the ministrations of dying. The Reverend accepted little Maurice's doom long before it was inevitable. Rev Grayling's efforts to help Maurice die were undermining Dr Higgins's to help Maurice live. In the end, with God on his side, Rev Grayling prevailed. How could he not, given such a powerful (an all-powerful!) confederate?

I tried to speak to you about the battle that was being waged in our very house, joined about Maurice's weakening body—but I only half understood it myself at the time, and you did not want to discuss Maurice and his deteriorating condition. You tended to him as a loving father but it was as if you were trying to render it unreal by not acknowledging it in words. Words have the power to create reality, so you avoided casting the deadly spell. So it seems in reflection.

I willed myself not to reflect on these unpleasant recollections and to concentrate on the conversation Mr Smythe and Mrs Shelley were having, largely about books, and specifically at the moment mythology: the story of Erebus, the darkness born to Chaos, along with Erebus's brother Night. I wondered at Mae's ability to compose herself after the disappointment of her thwarted rendezvous with her husband—but little by little I had sensed that living with the caprices of a poet must not be the easiest situation, and Mae had already grown inured to the twists and turns, the erratic highs and lows. Or, at least, she had already developed the talent for appearing hardened to them. Perhaps it was a kindred skill to her ignoring her son's worrisome congestion.

I am afraid my need for sleep has overtaken me, my dear. There is not much left to say regarding the diminutive *soirée*. I shall see about posting this on the morrow—or holding on just a bit longer (to fill the space remaining on the page). Good night for now, my love.

Sept 17—I now doubt this remaining space shall

suffice; in fact I know it shall not. So much has transpired. Our day began in the usual manner, and Mrs O
was just clearing the breakfast dishes when there was a
knock at the door—quite early for a visitor, especially
to our front door. Mrs O's hands were occupied, so I
indicated I would see to the caller myself. There stood
crimson-headed Katy, Mae's hired girl, and she had a
most worried expression on her ruddy countenance. I
found that I was not wholly surprised to see her, and
I suspected the worst. 'Missus has asked me to fetch
you, mum. She apologizes at the early hour but does
n't know who else, mum'. I told her I understood and
turned to get my wrap and bonnet. As we hurried
on our way I asked the girl if it were about the baby,
William. 'No, mum, missus herself is very poorly'. I
thought then about how Mae had appeared flushed
the day before. I was so preoccupied with William's
coughing and all of its painful associations, I barely
took note of his mother's health. I suppose I dismissed
any irregularities to her disappointment at missing
her husband.

We soon arrived at the Shelley residence and entered
through the street-facing door. Immediately I heard
William crying and coughing, practically choking in
his nursery. Meanwhile I spied Mae on the floor but
sitting with her back against the low seat of the settee. She was conscious but pallid, as pallid as a marble
bust. I knelt beside her. 'Thank you for coming, and
so expeditiously', she said taking my hand. Hers was
cold and moist with perspiration. She seemed barely

able to summon enough breath to speak. 'I must have fainted . . . I found myself here . . . I recall sending the girl for you . . . then'. She indicated with the expression of her eyes that then she found herself on the floor. William had ceased his sobbing thanks to the efforts of the girl, Katy. I insisted that Mae remain where she was while I fetched her a glass of water. There was a pitcher and glasses on the table in the kitchen. She took several sips, which appeared to help; then she allowed me to assist her to a sitting position on the settee. 'Thank you. I feel much improved'. Some colour had returned to her ashen cheeks. I asked if she had been eating and getting rest—it can be difficult to take care of oneself when also caring for an infant. She assured me that she had, and was beginning to summarize her dietary activities—when she suddenly stopped speaking, in mid-word, and tears began streaming down her cheeks. 'What is it, Mae'? I was seated next to her and I began patting her hand, which seemed carved of ice. After a moment she dried her eyes with the lacy cuff of her sleeve. 'I apologize for my emotions, but I do believe I may be with child again. I was hoping to see Shelley so that I could communicate the news in person'. I asked her if she were certain, and she replied as all women would, I should think,—that she was as certain as was possible, at this early phase at least.

William had stopped wailing in the nursery but his persistent cough soon returned to punctuate the bleak moment. One should celebrate the coming on of a new life, I know, except circumstances do not always facilitate celebration. I knew not what to say other than, 'Shelley will be thrilled at the news no matter how the intelligence is delivered'. Mae smiled in a way that was difficult to interpret. On the small writing-desk in the corner of the room sheets of paper lay ready for inditement, next to pen and ink-stand. The topmost sheet had received some writing. I could not determine, however, if it were the beginnings of a note to Shelley or an attempt to create the story she was determined to bring into the world, though she knew neither its facts nor its form, neither its moral nor its mode.

Since the girl was busy with William, I took it upon myself to prepare a simple repast for Mrs Shelley. Now more than ever she needs to keep up her strength. The Shelleys' larder was meagre indeed but I managed a bit of cheddar and a piece of bread soaked in what remained of some poultry broth, and a cup of thin ale which Mae had on hand. I could tell Mae was self-conscious of their Spartan existence—and to assure her it was no matter to me would have only called further attention to the situation. Mae was soon improved, so I left her in the care of the hired girl and (I was assured) the soon-to-arrive cook, whose charge it was to restock the pantry. I fear this last part is more the budding author's fictive invention than tangible fact.

On the way home I imagined that practically everyone I encountered was a deputized agent on the watch for Mr Shelley. I wondered where he kept himself, out of view and away from the debt-collector's clutches. How tempting it must be to slip away, to the Continent or America or even the Orient—someplace where one can begin again, reborn into a life free of past calamities, where old woes do not cling like thistle down. But of course Mr Shelley cannot: he has a wife (a pregnant wife!) and sickly child. Familial love and obligation root him here, on England's sandy and sullen shores.

I regret concluding on such an unhappy topic, my love, but my ink runs low—as does, I fear, your patience with this lengthy letter. I shall prepare it for the evening post.

So Looking Forward
To Your Return

September 18, 18—

Dear Philip,

An interesting day and it is not yet through. Mrs O'Hair had suggested some time ago that the downstairs rooms could benefit from a thorough cleaning—and there was no question that she was correct. At her age I was not going to allow her to try to shove the furniture here and there, roll up the rugs, and—most tedious of all—carry stacks and stacks of books. Not by herself certainly. I figured that the two of us together would be equal to the heaviest tasks, and with the enlistment of Felix and Agatha for the light work of odds and ends: It seemed a manageable operation. I knew that Robin was about but I did not want to superimpose upon him role of hired man. It seemed the sort of work that was beneath ship's captain, and perhaps I did not want to infringe on the dignity of my brother due to my own ego. I take pride in my brother's rank and enjoy the notion that his station is superior to the meanest of manual labor. Before you become excited at the idea of your wife's silliness be assured that my musings proved moot. We were only just beginning when there was a knock at the door which proved to be Robin's mate Mr Andropov. My brother must have been expecting him, listening for him even, for Mrs O had only just opened the door when Robin came down the stairs. My brother could immediately sense that something was afoot—no doubt his deduction relied much on my appearance: I was wearing my oldest and lightest frock, with the skirt tied up so as not to sweep the floor, and also my hair was bound back in a cloth to cool my face as I knew the work would warm me. To give the digested version of the tale: My brother and his mate insisted on lending their hands—and backs!—once they discovered what we were about.

I believe Robin and Mr A enjoyed the work. My brother certainly appeared in freer spirits than I have seen him for some time. He and Mr A even taught us a chanty by which to work. At first it was only to amuse Felix and Aggie, as they transported stacks of books here and there and back again, but soon Mrs O and I joined our voices to the hypnotic song, the chorus of which chimes in my head still:

> *Stand tall the beauties of Barbados,*
> *Young wenches, women and widows—*
> *Cock their backs and toss their heads.*
> *Up at daybreak, all, early from their beds,*
> *To haul their nets and pull their plows.*
> *Stand tall the beauties of Barbados.*

Seeing the ease with which Robin and the Russian fell into a working rhythm, I can understand how they survived the Polar wastes. When it came to the task at hand, they quickly seemed to be of one mind and one body. I comprehend how a crew, under the correct leadership, can become a single organism managing at once many tasks. In no time at all the parlour, hall, foyer and kitchen were dusted, cleaned, oil-rubbed, and reorganised. The windows, too, received an enthusiastic washing and the fireplace grates a good brushing. Floors, walls and doors—even the stairway banister was not overlooked. The thoroughness of our assault downstairs served to emphasise how much the upstairs rooms need an equal application of industry; however, that must wait for another day. Our merry crew was well worked by the time the last piece of furniture was returned to its place and the final book found the apex of its rightful stack.

All along, Mrs O had a large pot of stew simmering (its savory aroma, laden with thyme and rosemary, had been driving us to distraction), and she turned out a fresh pan of biscuits. Robin and Mr A were so famished it was a simple task to convince them to sit and sup' with us. I considered a leaf in the table but opted for a pleasantly full arrangement instead. Mr A appeared to expect the saying of grace—a ritual which has remained unobserved in your absence—so I invited him to be its orator. The children recalled the custom and went along without question. Mrs O possibly appreciated its unanticipated return. She had filled

our bowls before we were seated but there was still the
passing of the biscuit plate in addition to the butter
crockery and the jam jar, and the mortar of salt. I was
concerned that the children would find Mr A's hand,
with only its finger and thumb, disconcerting—they
were of course familiar with the Russian before today
and had now worked alongside him for several hours,
but it is one thing to be aware of one's deformity and
quite another to receive the biscuit plate from a muti-
lated appendage. Nevertheless, they seemed unaffect-
ed. Perhaps their own exhaustion and hunger made
them less prone to over-reaction. At first I had difficulty dislodging my recollection of the disquieting
dream which featured Mr A and the children *in this
very room, on this very table*. However, it turned out
that the Russian has an amiable and loquacious per-
sonality—thus the vigorous conversation soon swept
away the lingering cobwebs of the dream. I hoped Mr
A may begin to illuminate the chronicle of his and
Robin's Arctic adventure. He adroitly circumvented
the topic (no doubt knowing his former master's preference for a different subject), and instead spoke of
his travels before signing onto the *Franklin*. He is, after all, significantly my brother's senior and was a seasoned ship's carpenter before answering Robin's notice
for crewmen.

Mr A recounted many of his ports of call, and the
strange customs he associated with each. Felix and
Agatha were visibly spellbound by the stories, and Mr
Andropov's easy manner of recounting them; I dare-

say his accent added yet another layer of the exotic to his artfully spun tales. As Mrs O was pouring fresh tea, she asked, 'Of all the places you 've traveled, Mr Andropov, where pulls you back most magnetically'? I presumed it would take a moment's reflection before he could supply a response, but just like that he said, 'America. I have visited the great whaling port at New Bedford and spent a holiday in Boston—I would be pleased to return to either, but the place I truly want to set foot is New York City, and to travel via the Hudson waterway to a valley so enchanted and verdant that an old mate, when I was first apprentice on the *Cornelius Green*, could not cease speaking of it'. I had not expected such a precise and whimsical reply to Mrs O's interrogatory. Perhaps one day, my dear, when the children are raised and independent, you and I shall stoke a wanderlust and visit such alien places. Mr A's zeal certainly paints America with the rosy aura of a polished apple. Throughout, Robin had practiced a perfect but polite taciturnity, and I wondered if it were his friend's stratagem to carry the weight of conversation singlehandedly, knowing my brother's preference for silence.

Our leisurely meal at last came to a close, and Robin and his garrulous companion left the house to commence whatever had been their original design. I was going to assist Mrs O in the putting to order of the kitchen; however, she insisted that she complete the task herself as I looked most in need of rest. I could not disagree with her assessment. I wondered at her

own boundless energies. She does not seem emblematic of her race, the infamously slothful Irish. Then
when I consider the Irishfolk that I know personally,
none fit that disagreeable description. Perhaps some
have been in England long enough to amend their na-
tive-born inclinations.

I lay down for a rest and fell fast asleep for more
than two hours. I was most disoriented upon waking,
not knowing whether it was morning or night. I lit the
candle by my bed and even reading the clock on the
bureau did not help for a moment; then I recalled the
events of the day and concluded that it was six in the
evening. The house was supremely quiet. I freshened
myself and took up the pen to compose this letter. I
write with the petite secretaire over my legs, sitting in
bed, propped against four pillows. I must look the part
of a paragon of leisure, a lady of independent means
who has no care but to scribble her time away. I meant
to check on Mrs Shelley but alas the day escaped me,
with our herculean cleaning and story-filled supper.
The girl, Katy, did not bring news of further calamity,
so perhaps all are well on Marchmont Street. I hear
stirrings downstairs; I shall close this writing for now,
my love, and rejoin the world—though it may be that
it does not miss me.

I return. We spent a pleasant enough evening—
though everyone, including Mrs O'Hair, was feeling the depletions of exhaustion. Before retiring, she
spoke to me regarding a serious subject. With the arrival of Robin and a sudden spate of visitors, we have

been going through stores more vigorously than has been our custom. It has not helped that the weather has been unseasonably cool and damp; and I suppose as Felix and Agatha grow their appetites naturally increase, too. Whatever the specific causes, it seems we could use a slight increase for household expenses—I am certain it is quite temporary. Soon Robin will find a position (or perhaps chronicling his adventure will result in some modest income); moreover, the parade of visitors will reach its terminus, and we shall retreat into our more solitary lifestyle. I assume you are, by necessity, in regular communication with your employer. I hate to ask, my dear, but might you say something to Mr Pfender regarding a slight increase? I am confident he understands the difficulty of your living away, and on *his* behalf primarily. Or if such a request is not advisable at this time, perhaps you could send a note directly to Mr Peacock, directing him to increase the monthly allowance—to hold not quite so much of your salary in reserve. I appreciate the prudence of laying away for a stormy day, but of late it has begun to drizzle. Meanwhile, Mrs O and I will do our part in expanding only in the department of frugality.

In the spirit of said frugality, I shall hold this letter until tomorrow's second post, so as not to waste this page's space.

Sept 19—I slept soundly thanks to yesterday's exertions. The only negative is that Morpheus' deeper realm must be the region of especially strange and vivid dreams—not incubi by any means, but rather dreams embroidered with a fringe of weirdness. I hardly have time or space to describe them all here (in the hopes of providing you some amusement); however, I shall remark on their common theme: In each case, there was great emotion regarding something's arrival. I write vaguely 'great emotion' because it was not precisely the same emotion in each scenario. In one instance there was ecstatic excitement at the idea of the thing's arrival; in another sublime trepidation; in another soul-wrenching sadness; still another tear-provoking frustration; and so on. Moreover, I must write 'the thing's arrival' because it was consistently unclear as to what was imminent. Perhaps at times there were hazy hints as to its most basic nature but no clarifying details whatsoever. One would think that the accretion of enigma, the compounding of mystery would itself cause especial consternation. That was not the case. There was certainty that the thing (whatever is was) would arrive—that the supreme secret would be revealed: It was only a matter of time and of patience.

I want to believe the common thread was an omen of your return, my dear. I shall further hope this letter passes you en route. Perhaps you shall sense its presence in the northbound coach as you travel homeward on the road, southbound to us. I shall close on that happy thought and await the postman's midday visitation.

All My Love,

P. S. I shall not delineate upon it here, but we have just received that odd little man, Mr Havens of the Geographic Society. More to follow!

September 20, 18—

Dearest Philip,

Where to begin? It has been such a busy day! It commenced, as I intimated earlier, with a visit from the undersecretary of the Geographic Society, Mr Havens. I coaxed Robin from his room to see him. Normally I am disinclined to disturb my brother, but I must say Mr Havens bears the closest resemblance to an employer who has come calling for Robin since his return, and a source of income and a step toward independence would not be bad things for my brother; both, I believe, would be quite medicinal to his wounded spirit. I fear, however, that Robin suspects my design and is resistant to it. Nevertheless we found ourselves in the parlour with Mr Havens, in his tall collar and too-large coat with the padded shoulders, discussing matters further over tea. My sense was that Mr Havens was before us in a double capacity: As an official of the Society, he wanted to schedule Robin to present a paper before

the members—that much of the little fellow's enquiries was reasonably direct. Beyond that point his line
of thinking was not what one would call 'crystalline' in
its clarity. I shall not attempt to transcribe the circumlocutions but rather shall paraphrase what I ultimately
was capable of gathering. Hence: In an unofficial capacity Mr Havens has approached a handful of publishing firms on Robin's behalf in hopes of securing
their interest in bringing out a book-length account
of Robin's voyage. Meanwhile, he seems to believe that
Robin's paper being delivered to the esteemed body of
the Geographic Society will add 'merit' and 'authenticity' (Mr Havens's words) to a book on the subject,
thereby making it more attractive to potential publish-
ers and, eventually, to the reading public. The paper
would almost certainly be published by the Society in
its *Quarterly Proceedings* and thus be in circulation as
a sort of advertisement for the longer work (once written, edited, and published).

An especially round-about discussion ensued regarding Mr Havens's role in this scheme. It appears he
desires to be a sort of intermediary or agent in securing a publishing arrangement for Robin. My sense was
he would prefer to buy Robin's manuscript outright
and at that point be done with my brother altogether, leaving Mr Havens free to secure whatever manner
of arrangement he is able, solely on his own behalf.
However, my further sense is that the strange little
man does not possess the means to purchase Robin's
narrative (although the worth of such a book is be-

yond my experience to calculate). Thus he is left the arrangement which he has (seemingly) proposed.

I was surprised that Robin was more animated than he had been upon the undersecretary's first visit, actually asking some questions and expressing a modicum of interest in perhaps writing something about his expedition. To be clear, what I mean is, Robin did not reject the notion out of hand. Mr Havens attempted to pin him to a precise date by which time he may have a brief paper prepared for presentation, but Robin was unprepared or unwilling to commit to a precise date. In these discussions one cannot escape sensing the undercurrent of disappointment that Robin and his crew did not reach the Pole. Things would be starkly different then. I sense it too even though, at the same time, I find it grossly unfair to regard Robin's achievement and survival as anything less than a pennant-waving success.

At last, Mr Havens placed his tall hat on his low head and departed, feeling perhaps he had made some progress in executing his design. (I hope for his sake that his plan is plainer to him than he is able to communicate it to us.) I must acknowledge I felt a glimmer of optimism at the prospect of Robin's invigorating himself and possibly turning his project into some pecuniary gain. After Mr Havens left us, Robin surprised me regarding the prospect of seeing Mrs Shelley. It seemed he had read her brief narrative about the Arctic explorer and had some thoughts to share. I did not want Robin's unexpected enthusiasm to socialise to become extinguished, like an untended ember, so I sent Mae a note communicating our intention to visit in later afternoon.

Arrangements made, Robin and I went about our midday duties. I hoped he may retire to his room and begin work on the Geographic Society paper, but instead he took up a book from the hall and proceeded to the alley with a chair to read by sunlight, though it be filtered by gauzy grey clouds, the sort that are said to be unique to London. Eventually the hour arrived for our visiting the Shelley residence. I thought we may have a pleasant chat on the way, Robin and I. I did not expect him to confide any details of his adventure but maybe something regarding Mr Andropov's and his rambles in the city. My brother, however, was mainly taciturn during our walk. Occasionally he would make a random observation about something in our immediate vicinity—perhaps sensing the pressure to engage in at least the tiniest of small talk. We passed the vendor of spiced meat and Robin commented on the delectable quality of his wares. I of course pretended no familiarity with him and his cart. I thought the bearded vendor cast a knowing eye upon me as we strolled past. Robin's and my halting discourse about almost nothing caused me to reflect on our childhood, and I recalled with irony the times I became irritated with my little brother's perpetual chatter as he was inclined to share with me every thought which came into his head, or so it seemed. If I could transform him into that loquacious lad again, if for only an hour's time, he would confide in me all that I longed to know. Perhaps some small details would be revealed during his conference with Mae. I kept my proverbial fingers crossed. (I shall keep you in suspense, my dear!)

At the Marchmont house, the hired girl, Katy, responded to our knock, and I feared Mae was unwell; Katy, however, commented that her mistress was just finishing dressing and would be with us momentarily, as she encouraged us to take seat. Katy was bringing the tea tray when Mae emerged from an anterior room and joined us. Robin stood of course and took her hand as she sat in the chair adjacent the settee. It was the briefest moment, but I sensed something between Mrs Shelley and Robin. To call it a 'sympathy' would be fair, yet it was something more—a 'perfect sympathy' would be fairer but still not the thing precisely. There was recognition between them, as there *would* be since they had met previously at Mr Smythe's; it was not, though, the recognition of casual acquaintances—more like the reunion of dear friends who only this moment realised their friendship. Or, better, like longtime correspondents, letter writers of the most intimate and heartfelt secrets who have finally, just this second, met in person—and, especially, if the meeting were by accident, because, indeed, there was an element of surprise in both their demeanors.

I know, I know, my dear: I am allowing my pen to run off with my imagination, like a giddy schoolchild who has been freed from his fastidious tutor, but I swear I am doing my level best to describe the extraordinary moment as genuinely as I am able. I must acknowledge that I thought what a shame it is that Mae is already a married woman, for the bond between Mrs Shelley and my brother appeared at that instant unbreakable.

Aggie is asking for me, and I have been lost in writing long enough for now—

I am anxious to continue my narrative of our visit with Mrs Shelley, but in the meantime I have experienced a most disturbing episode. About an hour ago I went into the kitchen to speak with Mrs O'Hair and she was not present. I looked through the kitchen window and saw her with Bob, the coalmonger's man who I believe is sweet on her. They were just concluding their conversation apparently, and, to my surprise, Mrs O removed some coins from her apron pocket and handed them to the fellow, presumably in payment for the hods of coal he had delivered. The thing is, I had not given any money to Mrs O, thus my first thought was that she had helped herself to the keepsafe box, which is still in the closet beneath the stairs, tucked inside the old wool blankets. She had never been so forward (not to my knowledge at least). I did not want to confront her on the matter until I was certain of course so I straight away went to the closet to take an accounting. I was certain of its contents and keep the ledger as you have shown me. I counted thrice and every penny was there—it is not so great a sum that one would be easily thrown off by the figures. I could reach only one conclusion: Mrs O had settled with the coalmonger using her own modest means, a thought far more troubling than the idea she had helped herself to the keepsafe's contents. Then I wondered if she has paid any other bills on our behalves, which in turn makes one wonder *who is keeping whom?* I must speak with Mrs O'Hair of the matter. At first my thoughts were too scattered, I was too agitated. I have since managed to calm myself, but she is taking her afternoon rest. The moment must of course be right, with Felix and Agatha away and occupied. The episode does perhaps add underscoring to the topic of my previous letter: your contacting Mr Peacock about increasing our allowance. I have felt spread a bit thin, but maybe I underestimate the thinness if Mrs O has been augmenting our funds—it is almost too embarrassing to put on paper.

I shall attempt to distract us both from the unpleasant picture by returning to my description of Robin's and my visit to Mrs Shelley's. After the usual pleasantries and asking after Mae's health (cryptically avoiding the specific topic of her pregnancy in front of Robin), it was my brother who rushed headlong into the subject of 'The Mariner' (for that is what Mae has temporarily titled her tale). Robin began by expressing his admiration of Mae's writing style, her 'eloquence' and 'impressively developed vocabulary'. He also complimented her 'attention to details'. Mae thanked him for his kind words. On the one hand, she appeared quite pleased to hear his praise (she was, by her own characterization, an unpracticed story-writer); but, on the other, she seemed to be holding back her impatience for hearing something truly useful. Robin must have sensed it too for he curtailed the accolades and cut to the constructive criticism. He felt that the camaraderie of the captain and his crew was idealised; in fact, there is much 'quiet discord' onboard ship. 'Friction', he said, 'is inevitable, especially when navigating into unknown dangers. Second-guessing orders is bound to happen—but, yet, must not be tolerated'. What is more, Robin felt Mrs Shelley's captain confided too much to his first-mate. 'Even to one's most trusted crew member, one must trust very little'; then he added, 'There are few more isolating positions one can accept than ship's captain—perhaps lighthouse-keeper'. Mae, in spite of appearing a touch wan, seemed to be eager to hear Robin's critique. Robin gave her some suggestions regarding nautical terminology in her story—all of it lost on me of course—and that concluded his review of her manuscript. Whatever hope I had of learning something of substance about my brother's expedition was dashed. Mae had asked some clarifying questions, which Robin patiently answered. Then they were silent. It was not an awkward silence, however. It was the silence of the oldest of friends who required nothing further from one another than each other's close proximity. The silence of siblings, even, who naturally knew the other's thoughts. At that moment I felt that Robin and Mrs Shelley were closer, more kindred, than my brother and I had ever been, and may ever be. I must admit to a prick of jealousy,

but to my credit only a few seconds' worth. I told myself it was a product of my imagination: their silence
was simply that, silence—and I broke it by asking after
William's well-being. I had not heard him during the
whole of our visit. Mae said her little boy was napping. The doctor had visited and given William a nar-
cotic so that he could sleep peacefully—his incessant
coughing had been preventing his rest . . . it had been
preventing everyone's.

It seemed an opportune moment, then, for Mae to
get some rest as well, and Robin had concluded his
critique of 'The Mariner', so shortly we said our fare-
wells.

Yet another occasion had come and gone whereby I
hoped to gain some substantive knowledge of Robin's
adventure, and I came away with less than a morsel.
On our return home I considered asking him directly;
however, I knew its purpose would be to satisfy my
curiosity and not to relieve my brother of any burden
of withheld memory. I avoided bluntness yet afforded
Robin several opportunities to enter upon the subject of his own accord—thanking him, for instance,
for the good service he had performed for Mrs Shelley and commenting on how fascinating his critique
had been regarding the dynamics and protocols of
captaincy. Robin was not tempted by the bait, though,
and walked home in near perfect silence. Around us,
the lamp-lighters were at work as night was falling on
the city like a metaphor for my waning possibility of
enlightenment.

It is midnight or later, my love. I have been writing for so long that my hand is twitching; there is a tingling pain from thumb to wrist. Yet I do not want to let you go. You seem nearly here with me, perhaps in the darkness just beyond the terminus of my candle-light. If the ink were dry, I would take this letter into my bed, to sense your presence on the page as I sleep and dream of your return. Instead I shall let the letter lie here, on the bedroom's small table, and return to you on the morrow.

It is now noontime, and there is much to report. Robin has gone off with Mr Andropov, saying he may be absent a day or two. I knew it was pointless to attempt to wrest from him his specific plans, but he did volunteer that Bristol was his destination. From that, combined with the accompaniment of his shipmate, I presume the sojourn has to do with the *Franklin*. I offered him some money for his traveling needs, which he reluctantly accepted, insisting he would pay back the money, that he would 'pay back everything'. Then I realised what a burden Robin must feel himself to be. I hope I have not planted that idea in his head. I suppose it is the natural feeling of someone who has always been an independent spirit. It was one thing to be a dependent of our Uncle—Robin was but a boy and Uncle's abundant wealth was everywhere on display. Turning up here, at his sister's humble home, penniless and beaten, in every meaning of the word, it would seem—that is another matter entirely.

Robin and his Russian mate departed quite early.

Even though my brother has been far from a lively spirit in the house, his absence was suddenly conspicuous. It seemed to amplify attention to your long absence, my dear, and to the emptiness of Maurice's room. I did not have long to dwell upon the quiet queerness, though, as we had a perfectly unexpected guest at our door—our alley door—not an hour after Robin's departure.

I had just gotten the children committed to their morning lessons when Mrs O came to me (I was upstairs) and said I had a visitor awaiting me—*in the washroom*. I assumed then it was a deliveryman come to collect his master's due. There are several credits outstanding . . . all reasonable, my dear, all associated with the normal running of a house . . . but I felt a moment's concern as our current coin on hand is significantly depleted, especially after insisting that Robin take something for expenses. Rest assured I have been keeping the ledger religiously and felt certain no one would come calling for payment until after receipt of the month's allowance.

Considering all of this on my way downstairs, I am afraid I raised a bit of pique toward our visitor and was on the lip of setting matters straight when I opened the washroom door—and beheld Mr Shelley! I knew right away from his attire he was not a delivery fellow; nevertheless it required a moment for me to place him precisely. He has grown a beard, thin and patchy, since last I saw him; and there was generally a different look about him. I would have expected him to look a good

deal haggard, on the run as he has been from the debt
collectors, but, in fact, he appeared better rested and
better fed since our meeting at Mr Smythe's tea. Wherever he has been hiding away, it has agreed with him.

He began by apologizing for his intrusion and soon
came to the point of his surreptitious visit: He was
hoping I would deliver a letter to his wife. I wondered
then if he had learned of her situation. I wanted to
make everything plain but dared not violate Mae's
confidence. I assured him that I would be the bearer
of his correspondence, which he emphasised must be
done in secret. He was confident he had reached our
house without detection and did not want to draw attention to us. He made it seem his concern was on our
behalf, but I am certain he did not wish to compromise
a promising conduit of communication. He handed
me a sealed letter. There was a distinctive signet ring
on the hand which proffered it—no doubt the signet
impressed to the seal of scarlet wax on the letter.

He took up a dark cloak which he had loosely folded over the washroom bench (I had not noticed it) and
put it on. Before exiting into the alley he pulled up the
cloak's priestly hood—he was thoroughly concealed
and might have been any tradesman or cleric on the
street. Perhaps I am mistaken but I had the distinct
impression that Mr Shelley rather enjoyed sneaking
about and arranging clandestine contacts. It was all
thoroughly dramatic—theatrically dramatic, in fact—
which appealed to his natural character. If I were correct it rather irked me. There was poor Mary, dealing

with a sickly babe and her own compromised health, barely a morsel in the house to eat, and the additional burden of trying to write something which may sell and lessen the burden of her husband's financial situation. Meanwhile he is doing quite nicely for himself and enjoying the role of fugitive like a child at play.

I know . . . I must not leap to conclusions (I can hear your saying it, my dear). Perhaps Mr Shelley is laboring to repair his finances while feeling the pain of separation most acutely, and his tactics of obfuscation are sage precautions under the circumstances.

I was left then with a task I had not anticipated being part of my day. The children were fully engaged in their lessons, so I informed Mrs O I would be out but planned to return by mid-afternoon, if not sooner. I did not state my destination. The streets seemed unusually busy. I maintained a brisk pace, though I was careful not to appear that I was rushing. I felt that there were Argos' hundred eyes upon me. I knew it to be supremely irrational. Who would be watching me? What agents would be keen to my course? Though it was silly, I stopped suddenly to peer into a shop window—as if some item arrested my attention—my true design was to glance behind and catch sight of those following or at least watching me. Of course no one stood out as such a malignant observer; yet I still felt eyes on my back. I gazed into the window, hoping its reflective properties would reveal whoever was directly behind me noting my every movement. Other pedestrians walked past, and beyond them beast-drawn conveyances passed each other in the crowded street, their drivers and passengers oblivious to my existence.

I turned my attention to my own reflection. It must have been due to a strange trick of the light but I could barely discern myself. The images of those beyond me were far more distinct; I appeared but a half-formed apparition, a partially rendered ghost on the shop-keeper's plate of glass. It was nonsensical, yet I felt the form of the letter in the pocket of my skirt, and I felt the flesh of my leg against which the letter rested—to assure myself the correspondence was real, that it had material substance—and, yes, likewise, that I was a corporeal being. For a brief moment I had the queer-est of ideas (you will laugh!): I thought perhaps I was only a character in Mrs Shelley's story, a mere projec-tion of her authorial imagination, and a minor player at that, a character barely upon the page.

I realised I *was* the object of someone's gaze. The shopkeeper was standing by his wares looking back at me (or the street scene beyond). In any event, the spell was broken, and I continued on my errand.

There was a sharp wind, sharp enough to be felt in spite of the tall, close-built buildings, and the close-ly crowded streets; it freshened the neighbourhoods, subduing for the time being the grit and grime, and the heavy scent of humans and animals. I was grateful to be experiencing it, like getting a sudden breath of the country's air. I did not mind then the task befallen to me and the feeling of watchful eyes everywhere. I did not realise what a suffocating sense I had had until I was suddenly breathing easier. Though it was not precisely my lungs which felt stifled: it was my spirit. I do not wish you to take this passage as complaint about my life at home, about my role as mother and wife and sister, and as lady of the house. Not in the least. I love my life and will love it still more when you return. But things have been weighing on me—perhaps I did not realise just how much until being caught in the cathartic breeze. I have tried to move past Maurice's death, for the children's sake, and yours, and my own. I did not wish to become a vortex of mourning and grief, projecting sadness and bitterness like dark rays from a black sun, casting everyone around in a gloomy twilight of shadows. But I think rather than moving past the loss of Maurice I have simply papered over the darkness, a darkness which has grown large inside of me, and it is a thin papery skin stretched over the waxing orb of grief. It must tear away entirely—it is inevitable—and the black rays shall burst forth with the intensity of an equatorial sun. Rather, though, it shall effect an awful eclipse, a terrifying midday night, for those unfortunate enough to find themselves in my declining orbit, in the fierce setting of my black sun.

I fear a similar fate for Mrs Shelley should she lose little William, even with another child on the way. There is no true replacement for a lost child. Each babe is dear but the void left by a lost one can never be filled; perhaps, at best, one can be momentarily distracted from the empty space. I note my repeated use of the euphemism 'lost'. Is it too painful to write

its antecedent? I do not believe that is the cause of
avoidance. Rather, invoking the word, particularly in
the context of losing a beloved child, is like uttering
a hex—the calling forth of Loss personified to enact
his terrible, malicious trick again. I do not like to acknowledge such a primitive belief, such an obvious
superstition—yet I cannot help sensing Loss's near
presence, his relentless watchfulness, his giddy eager-
ness. Perhaps it is *his* eyes which are always upon me.

When I arrived at the Shelley residence, Mae was
not there. Katy showed me in. A large-boned woman, who must have been the cook, was tending to little William at the moment. He was asleep in her lap,
but not peacefully: I could hear the wheezing labor
of his lungs. I placed Mr Shelley's sealed note on the
papers on Mae's small desk and asked Katy to be sure
her mistress was aware of it. The girl's complexion was
nearly as enflamed as her hair, and she wore the rings
of exhaustion beneath her dull green eyes. The stress
of William's illness, compounded by his mother's condition and Shelley's fugitive absence, has been extract-
ing a heavy tax from the entire household.

I left as quietly as I could. I recalled Mr Squire's book
emporium on Marchmont and wished that I had had
the forethought to bring two or three volumes with
me which Mr Squire may be interested in buying—
something to bolster our coffers until you have been
able to arrange a modest monthly increase. I decided to pay a visit to the bookshop nevertheless. I am
familiar enough with our collection that I could dis-

cuss some titles with Mr Squire and perhaps arrange a purchase or two without the items being in hand. That was my design at least. Before I could execute it something quite extraordinary took place—involving my brother and Mr Andropov.

I shall get to its narration forthwith. When I reached Mr Squire's shop, the disagreeable fellow was at his desk in the rear of the establishment sorting through stacks of books and having an animated conversation with a fellow leaning over the desk and attempting, it seemed, to write what the shopkeeper was telling him—perhaps his assessments of the volumes the fellow had brought to sell or trade. The bell tinkled dully when I entered but it appeared not to attract their attention in the least. I did not think it advisable to interrupt the naturally brusque book-dealer before hoping to strike an advantageous arrangement with him, so I decided to bide my time by browsing his selection. As you may recall, there is a long table before the shop's windows which face Marchmont Street. It is arranged with a wide selection of new arrivals, each with its spine facing upward.

I had just selected a volume of Swift to peruse when some voices from the street attracted my attention. Angry words were being exchanged but I could only sense their tone, not their meaning. The men who were having the spirited disagreement stepped into view. It required a moment before I overcame my disbelief: It was Robin and Mr Andropov! I spied them through the shop window, the Swift still in hand. It appeared that it was my brother who was in a fit of anger, and his friend was mainly engaged in calming him—to no avail, however. My brother uttered a final hostile phrase; then stormed off, gesturing that Mr A best not follow.

The Russian stood there a moment, considering his next course of action (I gathered), before turning and walking in the direction from which they had come. I returned the book to the table and exited the shop—I suspect Mr Squire had no idea I had been there at all. I wanted to ease Robin's agitation, of course, but at the moment I was most concerned about the affable Mr Andropov, who appeared utterly dejected and down-trodden after the unpleasant exchange with his former captain. The Russian is long of stride, so even though I was at his heel immediately I had to rush a great deal to overtake him on the street. I called his name but he did not take notice until I touched his sleeve. Then he instantly stopped and turned. Seeing me out of the context of my usual surroundings and wearing my bonnet, it took him a moment to recognise me. I informed him that I had accidentally witnessed the row with my brother, and I asked him if all were well. The walk was only moderately busy but Marchmont Street itself was a hive of activity with carts and wagons and cabs, more so than I have ever seen it. I had to raise my voice over the din. Mr A appeared at a loss how to reply, or even *if* to reply. Then: 'There is a tearoom in the next block, Mrs Saville. Would you care to speak there'?

I did not care for the appearance of it—I assure
you, my dear—yet I very much wanted to hear whatever the Russian had to say. Ere long we were seated
at a table with a white cloth and green velveteen run-
ner, awaiting our pot of Imperial. We had exchanged
pleasantries and I was beginning to think I would
have to remind Mr A the purpose of our parley; however, he began thus, 'Your brother is not pleased with
something I have done. It is perhaps appropriate that
I shall inform you, madam, as the deed concerns you,
at least indirectly.' You can imagine my curiosity as I
urged him to continue. 'During our journey Master
Walton was quite dutiful in writing to you, his only
family. Our route made posting the letters supremely
difficult—thus a great many of them accumulated. He
kept them stored in a box in his cabin.' I told him that
I had received only a half dozen letters from Robin,
and each quite early in the expedition. Our tea arrived
and we took a moment to prepare it before Mr A re-
sumed: 'Eventually we sailed so far north and so far
beyond normal sea routes, the *Franklin* superseded
every last vestige of civilization. Your brother continued writing to you, but there were no means to dis-
patch them—they accumulated over many months,
including during . . . the *strange* time.' The Russian had
paused before the descriptive utterance to search his
adopted language for the right word, and one sensed
he was dissatisfied with his choice. I asked him what
he meant. He delayed by stirring and sipping from
his cup. 'We had found someone, a man, a Europe-

an, marooned on the ice, barely alive and mad from
his long exposure to the desolation. I did not speak
his language, Swiss I believe, but your brother did—he
has an amazing aptitude for languages'. I did not con-
firm Robin's talent, though I wholeheartedly agreed.
I was spellbound and wanted Mr A to continue his
narration. 'Shortly after we brought the Swiss onto the
ship we became trapped on all sides by the ice, which
moves continuously according to sea currents which
are too complex to predict. We feared the *Franklin*
would be crushed by the sheets of ice, some of which
stretched for miles, farther than the eye can see'. At
long last I was hearing details of my brother's voyage;
the Russian could not speak quickly enough for my
tastes. 'If we were forced to abandon ship, we would
not have survived long on the capricious ice-flow—we
would either drown if the ice broke into pieces, or we
would die a long and agonizing death of exposure and
starvation. When a man is faced with such prospects
and it seems the Fates have conspired against him, he
loses himself, or rather his former self, and transforms
into a different being. It is as if one's life is a sort of
outer skin—what do the naturalists call it, an "exoskel-
eton"?—and one steps forth, leaving his old way of being, his old way of viewing the world, of considering
life and death, leaving it behind in a single, discarded
husk. If he survives he will grow a new shell, a new
skin—but it is impossible to step back into his former
way of being: *that* man is dead, *that* fellow did *not* survive'.

I imagined my poor brother facing those dangers, confronting mortality. The Russian's story explained Robin's metamorphosis. Mr A drank his tea in a way which suggested he wished it were something stronger. 'There is more', he said. 'With little to do besides wait for the mercurial ice to either free us or destroy us, your brother was in his cabin most of the time ministering to the stranger, who had recovered enough to regain his voice, but otherwise was bedridden. The captain had ordered regular reports on the integrity of the ship—inspections and measurements to determine if the ice was compressing the hull, or if the *Franklin* were holding her own against the all-encompassing sheets. So the first-mate and I visited the captain several times each day; the stranger was always talking, talking, talking in his strange tongue, which resembled something like French with German pronunciations. It must have been an enthralling tale he told because Master Robert was constantly at his desk writing it all down. He only paused, it seemed, when we interrupted with a report on the ship, a report in which he only appeared half-interested compared to the story the Swiss was relating. He lay in the captain's bed, emaciated and pale as Death, wild-eyed and impatient to return to telling his tale and unburdening his soul, it seemed. Meanwhile something was happening to your brother. We had already known hardships so his health and constitution were not perfect even before becoming imprisoned by the ice: However, in sequestration with the Swiss, transcribing

his story or his sermon or his confession, whatever it
was—it was taking a terrible toll on Master Robert.
Visit upon visit I saw him becoming more deranged,
more desperate, drawing closer and closer to his own
terrible end. I assumed at first the change was due to
the ship's peril and likelihood of our annihilation; but
eventually I came to understand his decline was connected to recording the Swiss's ceaseless monologue.'

Mr A paused to drink. I did not know what to say.
I was transfixed by the horrific image of my beloved
brother wasting away and slipping toward madness
in the isolation of his cabin, obsessed with the char-
ismatic stranger's words. I imagined them as a sort of
malignant incantation, a spell the Swiss was casting to
quicken Robin's demise.

'I believe', continued Mr Andropov, 'the first-mate
and I were of the same thought, that under normal
circumstances we would intervene to protect the captain, but given the probability that none of us would
survive, what would be the point? For my part, it was
not a conclusion easily reached. It weighed on my con-
science for what seemed to be days—though they all
melded into a single, seamless, purgatorial twilight of
waiting. The decision was made for me when the Swiss
succumbed to his weakened condition and passed
away. The captain did not report his death; rather,
the first-mate and I learned of it when we delivered
our regular report. Master Robert did not answer our
knock, so we let ourselves into his cabin, exchanging
looks, both of us fearing the worst. Your brother was

at his desk, insensible, his head in his arms, beneath
which was the collection of papers which detailed
the stranger's story. I could not say if it were a coherent narrative or the erratic ravings of a madman. The
Swiss was dead, we discovered; the captain had pulled
the blanket over his gaunt and haunted countenance.
Just then there was a shudder throughout the ship, and
a great groaning—the ice was shifting. It could not be
determined, however, if this movement would end in
our salvation or our doom. This had been a harried
and chaotic time, you can imagine, as we attempted to
brace the hull wherever it seemed weak, but without
any means to identify the weak spots with certainty.
The process had more to do with staying busy and
feeling as though one's actions have some bearing on
one's fate. The sudden shaking and shuddering, and
the moaning of the ice, like a great mythological beast
who is in the spasms of terrible agony,—it went on
and on for what seemed hours.'

I sensed the Russian was telling his tale for the
first time. It was as much about unshackling the story
from his soul as it was informing me about my brother's experience and explaining the disagreement I had
accidentally witnessed. As such, I was determined to
interrupt as infrequently as possible. I had copious
questions but kept them unspoken.

He continued, 'For much of this period of
nerve-racking uncertainty, the captain remained in
his cabin. At one point I went to make report to him.
Before knocking, I heard him speaking, as if in con-

versation. I thought perhaps the Swiss was not dead after all. If so, it would have been a Lazarus-like resurrection. Then I heard another voice, low and coarse in tone; the words were foreign or at least inarticulate. It was not the first-mate, nor the voice of anyone else among the crew of nearly forty souls. I stood without the captain's door, considering everything, hesitating to knock. Before I could decide my course, there was a tremendous quaking that rushed throughout the length of the ship, and I truly believed the Fates had chosen doom for the hapless crew of the *Benjamin Franklin*. I fell to my knees to pray to the Lord our Savior, and a new vibration came to me via the battered and braced timbers: The *Franklin* had found open waters. I hurried topside and confirmed that we were clear of the ice. The first-mate was ordering the sails trimmed to guide us toward safer waters— for there were still bergs all around us. Master Robin joined us shortly, and he appeared to have had an even closer brush with death than the rest of us. We all had considered Death closely; Master Robert had conversed with him'.

I must say, my dear, I was riveted by Mr A's tale, even though I knew, more or less, its eventual outcome.

'We still had a long journey and trials ahead before reaching the *Franklin*'s homeport, but we had escaped the clutches of the Polar region with our lives. In two or three days, when we were clear of the largest of the bergs and felt we could breathe a trifle easier, the captain officiated over the Swiss's burial at sea'. Impatient,

I suppose, I interrupted Mr A to remind him he had
yet to explain the argument I had witnessed, which
brought us here to this tearoom in the first place. I
told him that I was grateful to learn the details he had
shared, but my curiosity was still keen regarding the
other matter. 'As I said, our trials were not at an end.
We discovered the ship had been damaged by the ice,
and she was taking on water. I shall not linger over all
the specifics of our woeful odyssey, but to expedite my
story I shall say that it was several weeks before we
reached the whaling port at Disko Island. As you may
know, it has long been the custom of mariners to use
such ports as the depositing and retrieving point of
correspondences. Sailors will leave letters and parcels
with the station-master, and in return they will take
on any items bound for the compass point of their
destination. I believe it was our second day at Keker-
tarsok (?) when I found myself following the captain,
who seemed to be en route to the station-master's.
Under his arm he carried a thick package wrapped in
heavy, brown paraffin paper. He was traversing a narrow bridge over an estuary when he suddenly halted
and stared across Disko Bay toward the sea. He stood
there for some time. I had paused, too, not wishing
to disturb his privacy—he had preferred to be alone
most of the time since our escape from the ice sheets.
Suddenly he took the package in his hands and flung
it into the estuary. Then, as if agitated, he hurried on
his way. He had not noticed me. When I crossed the
bridge I saw that the package had landed in mud, just

above the waterline. The tide was low but rising. I am not certain why but I decided to retrieve the package. Perhaps your brother's actions appeared so impulsive I believed he would regret discarding it. I found a place where I could climb down the slippery bank and reach the package. It was more difficult climbing out of the estuarial basin than going in, but I managed it. On the bridge again, I examined the parcel, wrapped securely in the waterproof paper and tied with hemp. The captain's intention was to post it because it bore a clearly written address, your address: Mrs Margaret Saville, Coram Street, Kings Cross, London, England. And I knew precisely what he intended to send you: It was the Swiss's narrative he had so dutifully transcribed. I could not imagine why Master Robert had kept the manuscript through all of our trials, carefully prepared it to post, then at the final moment tossed it into the bay. The captain had not fully been of his right mind since our entrapment in the ice, so I dismissed his strange action to that cause, and elected to post the package myself. There was still a good chance we would not complete our return to England—the repairs we were able to effect on Disko Island were only the most emergent and superficial, much more substantial ones were required to make the *Franklin* truly seaworthy—and the captain's writing may be the only chronicle of our journey. I must say I was curious about the contents of the package and was tempted to read the manuscript and learn the stranger's story, but I would not violate the captain's privacy. Thus I went to the station-master's office and deposited the package to await the next ship that could advance it on its own journey'.

'No such package has arrived, Mr Andropov', I informed him.

'Yes, on our return from inspecting and assessing the *Franklin*—your brother has seemed to be in improved spirits—so I risked enquiring about the parcel (I have been curious), and it was then that the captain first learned of my actions. You witnessed his reaction'.

I tried to imagine what was contained within those papers that would excite such emotion. I thanked Mr A for confiding in me but I felt I had already been away too long—and I was anxious to see Robin, and perhaps speak to him about what had agitated him so. I left the tearoom and proceeded directly home.

There is much more to report, my dear, but I have already written through much of the night, and my candle is nearly spent—as is my hand—so I shall close this letter.

Forever

Yours,

September 21, 18—

Dearest Philip,

I must *implore* you to reply!

These many weeks I have been missing you, sensing your absence every day; slowly worry crept into my heart, too, to sit beside your absent figure. I have tried to dismiss it as frivolous, feminine fretfulness, and to prevent my overimaginative mind from fabricating all manner of dire circumstances to account for your protracted reticence.

However, after this morning's visitor I have leapt well beyond fretting and fully into the field of worry, which, I must tell you, is contiguous with a tract that can only be described as unmitigated terror. Your banker Mr Peacock paid me a visit about mid morning. I had forgotten the irony of the achromatic fellow's name, having met him on only one other occasion. His ashen complexion and uniformly grey suit were well-matched for his gloomy demeanor and message of menace. He wanted to call personally, he said, rather than send an assistant because the allowance he had in hand represented the penultimate payment if the account is not replenished. I insisted that his arithmetic must be in error—that you are always a paragon of care when it comes to household expenses, while also laying aside a rainy-day egg in the nest. Mr Peacock had no response other than to encourage an enquiry of Mr Pfender.

I am loath to add this inconvenience to your burdens, my love, but I am certain you agree it is a matter which warrants immediate attention. I shall conclude this diminutive missive to be sure to have it in the noontime post.

Your Loving
  But Fretful Wife

September 21, 18—

Dearest Philip,

The day's normal routines have calmed me somewhat. When I returned from my tea with Mr Andropov yesterday, I was not able to speak with Robin (to say what, precisely, is unclear) as he was not here. In fact he must not have returned until after I had concluded my letter writing and fallen asleep. Today he has not departed his room; I am only aware of his presence by the occasional creaking floorboard above. I have been away from writing to see to a visitor: Rev Grayling. And a most surprising—if not *shocking*—visit it was! I received the Reverend in the parlour of course, and he began our meeting by sliding shut the pocket-door. He explained he did not want others to hear our conversation, and I gathered that by 'others' he chiefly meant Robin. To cut to the chase: He was concerned about Robin, who, it turns out, had sought out Rev G after his argument with Mr Andropov, and had been with him until the earliest morning hours (I can attest the Reverend did appear exhausted, with dark, heavy bags beneath his eyes, and a sunken look about his whole sallow countenance). What is more, this was not Robin's first visitation to Rev Grayling since his return. Indeed, the Reverend's previous call upon me was initiated due to Robin's seeking him out at Great St Bart. 'I cannot break Robin's trust and offer any details regarding our conversation', said the Reverend, 'but Robin is profoundly troubled. His experiences at sea have caused him to confront the most bedrock elements of our faith, and his conclusions threaten to tear him asunder, to shatter his sanity.'

I related to the Reverend in brief what I had learned from Mr Andropov—and he confirmed the tale, more or less, implying there were additional details he was unable to disclose. Rev G conjectured it was the knowledge that the manuscript was still in the world and possibly making its way here which triggered Robin's impassioned reaction. 'Perhaps', said the Reverend, 'your brother was managing to slowly forget his encounter with the Swiss scientist, an encounter which led to Robert's coming face to face with Satan himself, or at the very least Satan's earthly agent. And now a detailed account of that horror is returning to him, like a terrible image which keeps forcing its way into one's thoughts, a nightmare which can suddenly assert itself in the full light of day.' I of course felt great sympathy for my brother's extreme agitation: There are few things worse than having one's mind preyed

upon by fretfulness and foreboding. Yet I also felt
great curiosity regarding Robin's intimate encounter
with evil. I knew Rev G had already shared as much as
he felt at liberty to divulge of his and Robin's private
counsels. I thanked him for the time and care he has
taken with Robin; moreover, I assured him I would
continue to look after my brother with even greater
diligence. I meant for the remarks to be his invitation
to depart (I was sincere in my appreciation of the Reverend's actions in the matter, but my thoughts were
scattered and I was feeling the leaden weight of exhaustion myself—I needed privacy to sort through all
that had come so suddenly to light); it seemed, however, Rev G had an additional issue to address: 'Surely',
he said, 'this matter makes radiantly clear the importance of God in our lives. When we turn away from
Him, we also abandon the vigilance required to evade
Satan's snares, to sidestep his cleverly lain traps, which
are set everywhere in our modern world, where for
many science has falsely replaced the succor of the di-
vine. It seems this new century has provided purchase
for Satan's cloven hoof from which he intends to em-
bark on a new epoch of evil'.

I thought only briefly. 'It appears to me, Reverend,
that there is evil to spare in every epoch, and the only
one who has looked away—who has turned a blind
eye—is God Himself. It is He who abandoned the necessary vigilance long ago'. My words were not calculat-
ed, and sprang forth quite effortlessly. They must have
materialised in my soul over time, like the drop-by-

drop forms inside of caves, and I have been holding them dear in my heart, knowing them by their feel without ever articulating them into the bright light of day . . . until that very moment. Perhaps Rev Grayling was a bit stunned by my response. Or he simply had nothing further to say. Momentarily he had collected his hat and was gone from our home.

I both desired to speak with Robin and feared it. My mind was aswirl with so many questions and so many only half-understood things, I hoped that if I spoke with Robin it would help me to sort through the chaos, and quiet my thoughts; yet I had no idea how to broach the topics with my brother and feared my bungled efforts would only exacerbate his own disquietude. Of late, I have often recalled the sad fate of Nathan Wadkins, the young man, the family friend, who returned from the war with the rebellious colonies in such a broken state: It was whispered among my parents and their circle that his life was ended by his own hand via a self-administered pistol shot.

I hear Robin's stirring as if he may finally exit his room.

Robin had been improving. The days of rest and nourishment and being among those who love him had had restorative effects. All of that, however, was undone in a single day! My brother—gaunt, haunted, ghostly in his pallor—descended from his room. I asked him to join me in the parlour, and requested Mrs O to bring him a bever of tea and biscuits. He did not object; he seemed not to have the energy, nor even the will, to do so. The children had come to the parlour to do their lessons after Rev Grayling's departure, and I sent them away so that Robin and I could speak in private. Though they attempted to mask it, they again have grown wary of their uncle. I must acknowledge that I understand their trepidation. Robin and I sat, and he languidly fidgeted with the drawstrings of his shirt. I began, 'I have had conversations with individuals—' I stopped myself, deciding there was no purpose in circumlocution. '—with your friend Mr Andropov and with Rev Grayling. We are all concerned about you, my dear brother'.

Robin ceased his fiddling with his shirt, and I thought perhaps he was angry. He did not speak for a long moment; the tick of the mantel clock seemed suddenly thunderous. Then: 'There is cause for concern, my dear sister, but I should not be the focus of it. There are forces at work in the world which are very worrying indeed. My eyes have been opened to them, and it is difficult—nay, impossible—to shut them out again. Your home seemed so far removed, so insulated, I thought at first, hoped I suppose, it could serve as a sort of citadel. I knew I could not stay within its walls forever, but perhaps long enough to begin to forget, long enough to allow me time to find more permanent refuge'. Mrs O interrupted with the tea and biscuits. I thought Robin may decline them; on the contrary, he ate ravenously, and washed it down with a cup of still-steaming tea. I poured him another. He picked up the thread of our conversation as if there had been no pause: 'I have come to the realization that there is no insulated place, no walled city, no fortress . . . because the thing from which we seek asylum is in here'. Robin touched his breast. 'We transport it with us, carrying it inside whatever walls we uselessly erect around ourselves'. You should have seen his eyes, Philip; they were strangely calm but beseeching—as if he wanted me to refute him, to prove him wrong. He desperately desired to be in error. I, however, could not offer refutation. I suddenly felt that the walls of our home were paper thin and could fortify us against nothing. This house and all its contents were little more than a painted canvas backdrop on a stage—an illusion which could be dismantled by the facile manipulation of some ropes and pulleys.

Actually, not *all* contents seemed so unsubstantial and illusory: The books and the worlds they contained bore the weight of reality more so than the life I was now thrust into living. The books of course were everywhere around us in the parlour, and it was as if I could sense their multitudes of characters clamoring to burst forth from their bindings—they were literally *bound*—and assert their right to exist beyond the pages on which their authors had created them. They were alternate worlds more worthy than our own. I could not refute their claims any more sincerely than I could Robin's.

My silence had persisted long enough. Robin stood to leave the room (presumably to pursue whatever course I had preempted with my request to talk). Be-

fore turning away, Robin reached out and squeezed my
shoulder, a gesture of comfort before exiting the parlour and then the house. I had meant to comfort my
little brother, but instead I was the one who seemed to
be falling apart; or, rather, *fading away* may be a more
apt expression. I was reasonably calm (surprisingly
so), but I felt less and less like I had any influence on
the physical objects within my sphere. I could act; but
my actions had no agency.

After Robin had closed the front door behind him I
turned to a book which rested on the arm of the settee.
I wanted to be certain—I know it sounds ludicrous—I
wanted to be certain, so I reached out and knocked
the book onto the floor. I felt relief at the solid *thunk*
of its impact. I looked at it on the rug, fallen open to
its frontispiece and title page—Smollett's *The Expedition of Humphry Clinker*—and I am not certain what
I feared: that my hand would pass through the book
suggesting I am but an apparition, as substantive as a
shadow, or that I would discover the book was only
a painted object made to appear setting on a piece
of painted furniture, details of an elaborately evoked
room. I picked up the book, ran my fingers along its
cloth-covered boards, and placed it on the side table.
I saw that dust has already accumulated there. I used
my index finger to write my initials on the top of natural walnut, underscoring them twice: <u>MS</u>. They were
there, though barely discernible.

It came to me then that Mrs Shelley and I have the
same initials. It put me in mind of her; and with all

that had transpired, I had the impression I had not spoken with her in ages. It was hardly the case, yet the impression persisted, so I decided to pay a visit. Quite honestly: I felt that the drama unfolding under her roof would serve to distract me, for a time, from the one being performed beneath mine. Also, too, I was feeling a bit claustrophobic or agitated or both. I still sensed the multitudinous characters in the voluminous books advocating vigorously for their release. I thought at times I could truly hear their entreaties, like an overwrought mob demanding the reversal of some civic injustice. All in all, getting out of the house and calling on the residents at Marchmont Street seemed an imperative at the moment. I recalled the business I had hoped to enact at Mr Squire's and thought I should bring a book or two with me—but I did not wish to carry along the clamorous characters. Indeed, half the idea was to evade them altogether.

I hesitate to confess to you that which follows, but I shall . . . in an effort to be honest and forthright. No. If I truly wish to be honest, I must acknowledge that this would hardly be the first instance of my letters to you taking a turn toward the confessional, and such turns have not been exclusively in the name of connubial candidness. There has also been an element of relief, of unburdening myself from the weight of some selfish feeling, some self-serving thought. In that way, then, the confessional turns have themselves been selfish and self-serving. And thus the pattern perpetuates.

I did, as planned, ready myself and set out directly

for Marchmont Street. It was a sunny day, with a clear blue sky, and I realised just how long it has been that such weather has been seen in London. There even appeared a verdant splash in the neighbourhood, green grass at times revealing itself, and a late-blooming flower here and there. I wanted to believe it was an omen of some sort, that all the knowledge I had gained about Robin's voyage—and about Robin—was reflected in the clarity of the atmosphere; and that it was a sign better times were before us: I would move past little Maurice's death, my brother would find peace as well as a path toward productivity, and (best of all) you would return to the children and me; things would be placed in order once again.

Through all of the recent events I have come to understand just how disordered our lives had been and for how long. I have wanted to think of Maurice's death as *the* turning point, as the precise moment when day became night; but in fact his death was the exclamation mark at the end of a long passage of unhappiness and increasing episodes of gloom. Where, then, did that passage, that chapter, begin?—I pondered as I walked. Who can say with certainty? I think, though, of the argument we had about a fourth child. You seemed to have forgotten how difficult Maurice's birth had been and how relieved you were you had not lost us both—because he was still just toddling about the house and I had only just regained my full health (from my perspective), and you were insisting you wanted another child, to add a fourth mouth to feed, a fourth set of feet to shod, a fourth body to clothe. I had thought we were of the same mind on the subject, but then, suddenly, we were not. That disagreement placed us on either side of a divide which was untraversable. There was no bridge on which we might meet halfway, for halfway was a void, a free-fall into a bottomless abyss. That rift began the chapter which concluded with Maurice's devastating death—and I felt responsible. You had advocated for life; I for death—for what is *not-life* if not *death*? And it had been granted me. My position had won the day, and thus plunged us all into darkest night.

I had been so consumed by my self-critical reverie I arrived at the Shelley residence as if I had been magically transported there. I was inexplicably ill-prepared to enter the house, at least just yet. Also, it felt so, well, *good*, to be out—moving, thinking, observing—on this fine day. I wanted that feeling to continue. Mae was not expecting me, after all, so what would be the harm in delaying my visit a tiny bit?

With no specific destination, then, I set out. On the one hand, I did not want to stray too far from the Shelley home on Marchmont; on the other, how can I describe it? It was as if an invisible cord was pulling me to wander into unfamiliar parts of the city: To see what I might; to hear what I might; to smell; to taste; to, most of all, *feel*. Indulging the tug of the invisible cord, allowing it to take me where it may, gave me the sense that the urge, the inclination, has always been present, but I have ignored it, suppressed it even. I

suppose that is why I never questioned Robin's obsession with reaching the Pole, and his years of preparation aboard the whaling vessel. Not only did I not see
such actions as dangerous folly—I, at my core, understood them. I even (I can acknowledge now) envied
him them. If I had been his brother and not his sister, I
would have joined him in his adventures. Who knows,
being his elder, I may have led the way myself. Instead,
I played my womanly part, well taught by the world, to
encourage and to worry.

I do not wish you to think yourself deceived for all
these years, my darling. I can speak plainly of the feelings and thoughts now because they have only now
plainly revealed themselves to me. If I have deceived
anyone, it is myself. Can the emancipated genie be returned to his imprisoning lamp? That is the essence of
the question which asserted itself most persistently as
I rambled in the increasingly unfamiliar streets.

I turned in the general direction of the old industri-
al canal which I knew cut through that section of the
city. Why, I am not certain. I may have believed the
waterway would be scenically enhanced by the lovely weather. If so, my thesis was soon disproved. As I
drew closer to the canal, still out of view, the air became more and more tinged with the water's foulness.
It would seem to improve—that is, to be less powerful—then a sudden surge in the breeze would renew
with added intensity the olfactory assault. I came to a
busier block and discovered the reason for its tumult
of traffic: A slaughterhouse was the neighbourhood's

central establishment, built on the bank of the canal. Besides easy transport, the canal no doubt provided efficient deposit of offal and animal excrement. Wagons and carts bustled through the dung-filled street, pulled by beasts who perhaps wondered if they were being driven to their own destruction. Men's voices, mixed with the vocalizations of various animals, were as heavy in the air as the putrid odors, accented acridly by the lye which was intended to mask (to no avail) the other smells. Adding to the snarl of traffic was a wagon which had broken down in the street. Its pair of mismatched horses, a grey and a chocolate, had been unhitched and were standing, harnessed, some distance off from the wagon, where men had removed a wheel and were inspecting the wagon's rear axle. It was difficult to say if they were in the process of dismantling the conveyance or putting it back in order.

Overhead, the blue sky had become cluttered with clouds. One could almost believe the air around the slaughterhouse was so tainted it was capable of bespoiling the very atmosphere. I recalled the terrible noises to which I had awoke several nights previous: This place must have been the source of those nightmarish sounds. Normally the light of day renders ridiculous that which had terrified us in the dark of night. Not so with the slaughterhouse: If anything, the fully detailed daytime rendering revealed it to be even more horrific, even if that horror were only hinted at from the street.

I hurried from the scene, now beneath a sky whose

clouds revealed their bruise-coloured bellies. I had
tried to keep my bearings but I was already beginning
to feel disoriented—however, not in a frightening way;
rather, I was in an exhilarated frame of mind. In sum,
the adventure appealed to me. Frankly I could understand Percy Shelley's being attracted to a secretive,
cloak-and-dagger sort of existence. I could almost
forgive it—if not for the knowledge of how it affected
his family, especially poor Mary, who was not at liberty to simply wander away from her responsibilities,
who must in some ways feel shackled to them like a
common convict.

It was a relief to distance myself from the slaughterhouse, and for the air to clear of the stench. There
was a helpful westerly wind. The way was also clearing
of pedestrian traffic, which struck me as odd in the
middle of the day; then it occurred to me that perhaps
I was in a section of the city which came alive at night,
therefore whose inhabitants were, for all intents and
purposes, nocturnal. The buildings of besooted brick,
dotted with dingy windows, nearly all of which were
darkly curtained now, certainly bespoke of that sort of
neighbourhood. The area seemed abandoned but in
fact it was no doubt teeming with sleeping masses. I
thought of the thousands of dreams that played within
the squalid rooms, and of the daytime nightmares that
deposited their residue of worry and regret. Another
thought came to me, that the buildings were but set
pieces on an extravagant stage. I touched a patch of
rough brick to assure myself of its genuineness.

While I walked and mused, I became increasingly aware of the sense of being followed. It was different from the feeling of being watched, which had so affected me on my previous outing. There was an element of physicality beyond the idea that eyes were upon me. I turned a corner (into a particularly narrow street, I soon discovered), and instantly stepped inside a recessed doorway to use as a vantage point for my own observing. I was surprised when my pursuer proved to be pursuing me on four feet, or, more accurately, four paws: It was a lean but solidly built dog which came around the corner, some sort of mixed breed, a short-haired boxer or bulldog, broad-chested with a medium muzzle. It did not appear especially aggressive but at the same time I would not want a leg or an arm seized in its powerful-looking jaws. I hoped it was only coincidence that we were on the same route, he and I, and he would pass me by to continue about his canine business. However, he stopped short of my partly obscured place and was clearly waiting for me to make the next move. I stepped into full view and faced the brute. We made eye contact for a moment. Otherwise he did nothing, neither panting nor wagging his stubby tail.

I continued on my aimless path. After a time I looked over my shoulder, and my shadow had apparently grown bored and already wandered off after other more scintillating pursuits. I felt strangely alone, or, more accurately, lonely. It is not that I had formed an attachment so quickly to the stray dog, but rather his sudden absence drew a dark line beneath absences in general, like your absence, and little Maurice's. Then the irony struck me with force: Here I was wandering unfamiliar streets, heavy of heart for absent family, while voluntarily separating myself from Agatha and Felix, who are very much present in my world and would appreciate their mother's undistracted attentions. I resolved to pay my visit to Mrs Shelley and return to the children with all due haste. I soon had to acknowledge, however, that finding my way back to Marchmont Street was not going to be as simple as I hoped.

Rather than retracing my steps, I believed I could strike a more direct path (and avoid the slaughter-house), but the ancient streets ran at odd angles and half the time I felt I was moving away from my mark instead of toward it. I was mainly annoyed at the position into which I had managed myself; and I must own to a trace of panic as well—an emotion, though, which added an element of exhilaration to the predicament. I kept walking, intent on recovering my bearings. (I obviously found my way home, for I am sitting here recording the incident, probably in more detail than you would prefer, but the hour has grown late and I am exhausted from my excursion. I shall conclude for the time being before describing the most interesting episode of my Ulyssean wanderings.)

Sept 22. I presumed I would sleep soundly, from sheer exhaustion, but my rest was hampered by a host of unpleasant images and ideas, particularly of the man in green. I know my reference is obscure, my dear, and I beg your patience. After a few fitful hours in bed, I have given up on the hope of refreshing slumber and returned to pen and ink. I at least have some control over my ideas and images when writing—not so, at all, when sleeping (or attempting it). Before continuing in earnest I must apologise for the paper I am about to begin using. I had several sheets of writing paper on the table in my room; however, when I came home and eventually turned to the pleasant task of writing to you, I discovered most of the paper was missing. I shall get to the bottom of its disappearance when the household awakes. In the meantime, though, I have had to resort to the oddly cut scraps of butcher's paper the children use for their drawings. As you can see, it is serviceable but hardly ideal.

To return to my narrative of the streets, I was attempting to return to Mrs Shelley's on Marchmont but had become thoroughly disoriented among the weirdly angled thoroughfares, and was making as many false turns as fruitful ones. Foot traffic, by and large, had increased, and I counted that a positive. The negative, however, was that among the influx of pedestrians were those who appeared of questionable repute. Not to keep you in suspense, I soon sensed a familiar figure who seemed to be following me. You will recall the ne'er-do-well in the green coat who, along with his partner, were trailing after Robin, what?, six or seven days ago. When turning a corner I believed I saw the fellow, via a sidelong glance, recognizing the unusual colour of his cloak. Now my mind was divided: I was attempting to locate Marchmont while also determining if the pair of uncouth fellows were in fact following me; and if so, how to lose myself from them. This odd dance seemed to go on for some time, yet it was likely only a few minutes in duration.

In my confusion I entered what I discovered was an alley with no outlet. When I realised my error, I pivoted to return hastily to the street. It was already too late. The pair of ruffians had darkened the alley's entrance. We stood facing one another. Both men were coarsely bearded; the fellow in the brown coat was somewhat taller and leaner than his mate. I do not like to consider their possible designs. I hardly present the image of a wealthy lady who may have rubies and pearls on her person, thus I detest to even consider what their purpose in accosting me may have been. I can write calmly of the event now; however, I assure you that in the moment I was anything but calm. My mind was a maelstrom: Should I run? And run where? Should I shout out? Should I reason with them? Should I look for something in the alley to use as a weapon, a board or a brick? Et cetera, et cetera. My heart was racing inside my ribs. Before any frantic decision could be reached, the menacing growls began. (Not mine—although perhaps that may have worked too!) From behind me, I heard deep-throated growling and almost snarling. It was my acquaintance, the dog of mixed parentage, who must have been following me all along for he was there in the alley. *Caninus ex machina.*

Momentarily he placed himself between me and
the two men. The dog's bulk was magnified by his
intimidating vocalizations. The men had no interest
in any part of the potential exchange and turned on
their heels without fanfare. The dog ceased his menacing behavior as soon as the fellows exited the alley.
I risked scratching him between his upright ears, one
of which was creased by a scar. He expressed little interest in my gesture, as if his actions had nothing to do
with my protection, but rather were due to some score
he had to settle with the two brutes. I was grateful in
either case.

I returned to the street and before long found my
bearings. The dog did not appear to follow. When I
called upon Mrs Shelley, who was not expecting any
visitors, I caught her in the throes of writing. I felt terrible when I discovered that fact—we were in the front
room, and her writing desk was a tempest of pages,
most of which were black with tightly penned script
from edge to edge; and her fingers were stained by the
intensity of her literary efforts—but she assured me
she was most in need of a respite and my timing was,
in fact, flawless. She was still confused and conflicted
regarding the substance of her story, yet I sensed the
struggle with her narrative was in general beneficial.
She appeared haler than upon my previous visit, and
more cheerful. I suppose immersing one's self into the
lives of one's characters provides an interruption from
one's own trials and tribulations, at least temporarily.
(I can relate to that phenomenon even though I am

not writing a fiction; communing with you, my dear, via these daily missives affords a comfort which I cannot achieve through any other pastime—not reading, nor even my stitchwork, which I have not touched for days. Indeed, more and more I am reluctant to set aside the pen and re-enter my real world. Only the needs of the children, the demands of the household, and the throbbing ache of thumb and wrist prevent me from writing perpetually and passing every second with you here on the page.) Mae must have been still somewhat submerged in the narrative world she was creating for as we spoke she touched her cheek absentmindedly and left there a dark impression. My maternal instinct was to wipe it away but instead said nothing. It seemed in the moment a badge of distinction; besides, she would notice it herself soon enough.

I declined her offer of tea, explaining I had been out longer than planned and wanted to return to the children. I expressed my satisfaction at seeing her more vigorous before excusing myself from her home. She appeared to appreciate my visit, abbreviated though it was, if for no other reason than it provided her a brief break from the chaos of her composing. I have trouble relating to Mrs Shelley's dilemma, words tumble from my pen so effortlessly; but then again I am not attempting to create a whole fictional world—merely record real events and the thoughts and feelings they actually evoke. Our tasks, I freely acknowledge, are not the same. She is trying to envision a Versailles, to erect a stately edifice; I am simply constructing a common cottage, crudely hammering together a humble home.

Well, my love, this makes you current with our domestic affairs. Today has been quiet. The children are busy at their lessons—you would be proud of their efforts!—and Robin has spent most of the day engaged upstairs, which reminds me: The mystery of the vanishing writing paper has been solved. Robin was the culprit. He confessed as soon as he saw me this morning. He apologised for his forwardness, but I was not available to ask permission. It seems he has begun the report of his experiences for the Geographic Society—a 'brief account', as he describes it. I suspect that implies he will be omitting the more dramatic elements (as related to me by Mr Andropov), and focusing instead on the naturalistic and scientific aspects of his voyage into the uncharted. In any event I am pleased. I assured him that his pilfering was perfectly fine and understandable under the circumstances. I informed him we would visit the stationer and purchase more paper—though in truth we may have to postpone the acquisition until after our accounts have been augmented. I believe it is time for me to address this odd assortment of pages, seeing as how the postman shall arrive within the hour.

Your Loving
& Somewhat Fretful

September 23, 18—

Dearest Philip,

I am most intrigued by the letter which arrived in the morning post. It is addressed to Robin, and I am certain I recognise Mr Pfender's hand. I imagine I know its main idea, and I can only say thank you, my love. I am sure you placed the proverbial good word with your employer, and he has found a position to offer my brother. In your typically clever way you have managed to overcome two obstacles: provide Robin with a professional path by which he may support himself; and meanwhile his income will bolster our own accounts as no doubt he will want to contribute whilst he remains under our roof. I am equally impressed with the speed of the postal service, and must remember to praise our postman with the efficiency of his institution. I am already feeling the lightening of the load. I am perhaps pacing ahead of myself, but I know a good measure of the relief is sensing this contact with you,

my dear. Even though the letter is not from you directly, I can detect your arrangement of things, behind the
curtain as it were, and it must mean you have read my
tedious tomes and are reacting accordingly. *That* is the
real relief: to detect your presence in the works!

I am so anxious for Robin to read the letter and
set things in motion. I am tempted to rouse him, as I
used to do when we were children and my playmate
was inconveniently still abed. He would always be
grumpy until he had his porridge and tea, taxing my
patience as I anticipated our game. I remind myself
that his sleeping late is due, now, to his work on the
Geographic Society paper. I am not certain of the time
but I awoke in the night and peering into the hall I
noticed the light beneath his door. I wonder if he has
done much writing at all since recording the Swiss scientist's tale and then tossing it into the Greenland bay.
I imagine not. I must leave off for now. Aggie is asking
for my attention. Besides, I am too excited since the
arrival of Mr Pf's letter to concentrate.

Robin finally rose at about 10 (I may have curtailed
his sleep by choosing this morning to consider alternate arrangements for our room and dragging the
furniture about, here and there, and here again—and
the hallway did need a thorough sweeping, particularly just outside Robin's door). Whatever the cause,
he came downstairs and I promptly handed him Mr
Pf's letter (I nearly wrote 'your letter' for it does feel to
me like it has come from you!). I could not detect R's
emotions as he broke the seal and unfolded the cor-

respondence, which appeared to be heavy, expensive paper. He may have been excited or chary or wholly disinterested. We were standing in the well-lighted kitchen, but his emotions seemed obscured in shadow. He scanned the letter quickly before handing it to me—there was not much to read, only that Mr Oliver Pfender, Esq, requested Robin to visit at his office at my brother's earliest convenience to discuss a matter of importance. 'I suspect he must want to see you regarding a position'. I all but blurted. 'I do not understand why that would be *a matter of importance*', he replied. 'Besides, what sort of position would he have for a failed explorer, the captain of a battered ship'? 'You have manifold talents, many of them *unexplored*', I said—I must admit I felt a pinprick of pique at Robin's lukewarm reaction to the letter, and to the kindness I am certain you have orchestrated on your brother-in-law's behalf. Robin was more deliberate in his preparations than I would have preferred (I know we must be in a forgiving attitude given all that Robin has suffered) but in about an hour's time he exited the house to pay his visit to Mr Pfender.

I am awaiting his return, excited to know for certain what it is about. This act of kindness on your part has got me thinking of other such acts you have performed—like the time you arranged for me to visit Hassocks when we learned that Great Aunt Maribelle was gravely ill. You selflessly assumed my domestic responsibilities in addition to your professional ones; and when the presumed period of my absence stretched from a fortnight to a full month, you were not cross at all, insisting I must take as much time as needed to see to my aunt, and then to see to her interment. I know that it was a terrible burden for you (Maurice was barely walking at that point and still in his nappies), yet you cheerfully facilitated my protracted sojourn. I recall suggesting that we hire an extra girl to assist with the children, but you were determined it was unnecessary.

When I returned home I noticed the increased bond between you and the children; in fact, for a time I felt something of a carriage's fifth wheel—you had managed things so efficiently while I was away. I remember vividly the scene when I walked in upon my return and there you were, shirtsleeves rolled back, waistcoat unbuttoned, collar open, and little Maurice in your arms because he had awoken agitated from a nap. I tried to take him from you but he was reluctant to leave his father's protecting grasp. I recall, too, when we learned of Mrs Roberts's situation after her husband's sudden passing and their tangled mess of financial affairs; you volunteered your expertise in making sense of them and assisting the widow onto more stable footing in her grief. You were so discreet, not wishing to add embarrassment to her woes. Hardly a soul knew of your efforts to decipher her late husband's books and provide the young widow a clearer understanding of her situation. We barely saw you for weeks as you assiduously sorted through Mr Roberts's papers in the evenings after fulfilling your regular responsibilities for Mr Pfender. I know you took no pleasure in bringing to light Mrs R's desperate circumstance, which prompted her to abscond to the country, becoming a dependent of a distant cousin, if I recall accurately as you reported it. Poor woman.

Perhaps at times your natural inclination to be of help has been overwrought, like your volunteering to stand in for your colleague in the northern office when he suddenly took another position, leaving the firm in a difficult situation. I am certain Mr Pfender appreciates your sacrifice on behalf of him and his partners. No doubt that has made him pliable in regards to hiring Robin. Still, I believe anyone would recognise that you have done more than your part already—so I hold out hope he has bid you return to the home office (perhaps to oversee the training of your brother-in-law?). I know I must keep my wishes in check, yet it does seem to me that we are due for the gears and gyres of the world to fall into place to our benefit. Robin's return was the harbinger of just such an adjustment of the world's works; and in spite of the unsettling nature of recent events, I continue to trust that everything shall fall into place for our little family.

Now I must force myself to set the pen aside and see to the children . . . to wait for Robin's return, and the good news I am convinced he shall bear.

I look upon what I wrote only a few hours ago—can it be?—and am barely able to suppress my laughter. My optimism suddenly rings so naive—so *stupid*. I suppress the laughter which wells in my breast where the hope so recently collected, like life-giving waters from an unseen spring, because I do not want to frighten the children—for surely should I let it loose into the world, it would be the brittle and chilling cackle of an hysteric, the mirthless laugh of a madwoman. For mad I must be! The fact I now continue this letter must be accounted as evidence of my relinquished sanity. Yet what else am I to do?

It is wholly appropriate that as I write I again can hear the horrors of the slaughterhouse, brought, I gather, on a westerly wind—the animal vocalizations of fear and pain—because I am a kindred soul on this darkest of nights: I too have been prodded to my de-struction, torn asunder by a hand whose intent and motivation I have not understood, my ignorance ex-posing me, totally ill-prepared for the cleaver's stroke.

I must stop. I must stop. I must gain control of my faculties while the possibility still may exist. In a re-versal of roles, Robin has just looked in on me—now he is the fretful sibling watching over his playmate of old, performing the part of parent in their long-passed absence. I must attempt to record events in as objec-tive a manner as I can manage. Perhaps the mode of objectivity shall allow me to keep hold of whatever self-composure remains. I must curb the wild torrent of emotions and coax into calmer words what has transpired—and I may as well record them here, in spite of the medium's newest frock of futility.

I begin.

Robin had been absent nearly three hours when

he returned from his appointment with Mr Pfender. He entered with a sizable parcel under his arm; it was wrapped in heavy brown paper and tied securely with postal twine. Robin's demeanor was odd: something was weighing heavily upon him—which, yes, has more often than not been his state since his return from the sea, but this was different, a new kind of ballast had been added to his burden. My initial thought was that his cheerful mood (cheerful at having been offered a position by Mr Pfender) had been superseded by the unfortunately timed arrival of his package of un-wanted papers, which Mr Andropov had imprudently rescued from oblivion and sent on their way. 'Come, Margaret, you must sit', said Robin, directing me to the parlour, and ominously shutting the pocket-doors.

I sat (I do not recall where precisely). He did not let go of the parcel of papers, which struck me as strange. I was trying to think what to say to him about their arrival, how to rid him of the anxiety he was obviously feeling. 'How was your meeting'? I enquired, trying to distract him from the thing which he held securely be-neath his arm, almost as if trying to hide it from me. A foolish stratagem. Robin sat. (Mrs O'Hair and Agatha had baked a batch of biscuits with orange zest, and a citric scent filled the downstairs—I knew the tang of orange would forever make me recall this moment—I had that crystalline thought just then, as Robin seat-ed himself.) 'Mr Pfender did not wish to speak to me about a position. Something has transpired. It is not clear precisely what'. I did not know that one could feel one's face turn pale: another crystalline thought which formed. I gripped the arm of the settee (oh, I had selected the settee). The pattern of the cushions' upholstery is repeated on the settee's padded arms; I am not certain I knew that. Florals and stripes against a sickly yellow anterior. 'Philip is not in Dundee', said Robin in measured tones. 'We are not certain where he may be . . . if anywhere'. His voice trailed away. 'What do you mean? Explain what you mean'. We cannot hear ourselves accurately, but I am certain my voice was shrill—already hysteria was commencing its usurpation of hope.

Robin seemed to switch to his voice of command, perhaps automatically counterbalancing my turn toward the high-pitched with a captain's steely projection of emotionless control. 'I will explain, but you must try to remain calm. Nothing is certain. So there is no point in overreacting to something which only *may* be'. He placed the package on the tea table in front of us and untied the twine, but did not yet unwrap its contents. I saw that there were no markings on the brown paper, no address; and the parcel was in pristine condition: whatever the package was, it was not the bundle of papers Robin discarded and Mr Andropov surreptitiously retrieved from a muddy estuary. Robin said, 'Mr Pfender contacted me because he has not heard from Philip for weeks—for roughly the same length of time you have experienced his silence. Concerned, he wrote to the county constabulary requesting that they make an enquiry at the boardinghouse where Philip was lodging'. Robin removed a set of folded pages from his jacket pocket; I had been shocked dumb. 'This is the assistant constable's report. Allow me to read it verbatim: "Dear Mr Pfender, I called at Mrs Turnbull's of Fenton Lane and confirmed that Mr Philip Saville of London had been lodging there since the twenty-first of June; and according to the landlady, Mrs Alice Turnbull, a woman of sixty-some and an honest disposition, Mr Saville kept clockwork hours for the duration of his stay. She understood him to be a man of business, and he spent his days calling on various merchants and agents in the area; then he would spend his evenings recording in his books, usually burning a candle in his room quite late. She reported him to be 'a polite man, but quiet to himself—not inclined toward conversation at meals nor socializing with the other boarders in the evenings'. She further noted that he seemed dedicated to his employment but 'otherwise was not a happy man'. Then on the seventh of August Mr Saville did not appear in the dining-room for his breakfast. Mrs Turnbull assumed he was feeling poorly and was taking additional rest. When he had not risen by noontime, she made enquiry at his door. He did not respond. Always respecting the privacy of her boarders, she did not press further at the moment. However, when suppertime came and went, and she had heard no sign of Mr Saville, she elected to knock him up. When he did not respond, she entered his room to find it unoccupied. The bed was made, though it appeared he may have rested atop the covers. The room contained his personal belongings, except she believed some may be missing, for instance, the black boots he was fond of wearing and his familiar top-coat. Beyond those articles, she could not say with certainty. There was, and I quote, 'a singularly odd circumstance' for which she could not account. She could not fathom how or when he departed the house. She felt confident Mr Saville went straight away to his book-keeping after the evening meal, as was his unbreakable habit, and was in his room until all were retired, at which point the landlady made sure all the doors (three) were locked. She prides herself on the well-being of her boarders, and considers it her sacred duty to check the doors before taking her own rest. She is certain all three doors were securely locked on the morning after Mr Saville's disappearance, and moreover the window in his room was firmly latched. Again, she cannot say when or even how he exited her house. It must have taken place prior to her final check of the doors, although she cannot see how it happened as it was a memorable evening in her home—'a poet of accomplishment' gave a recitation in the parlour, and all the guests attended, save for Mr Saville. The unusual amount of activity in the house would have made it unlikely for him to leave without being noticed by someone'".

Robin paused and said, 'Perhaps the landlady was precisely mistaken; perhaps the increased activity facilitated Philip's leaving the house unseen. Or perhaps her memory is faulty, and she is confusing separate evenings'. Then he continued reading aloud: "'The room's rent was paid through the end of the month, so Mrs Turnbull left it undisturbed thinking Mr Saville may return. When he did not, she had his possessions moved to storage. She would like it duly noted that every item is accounted for and awaiting retrieval. She further reported that letters to Mr Saville continued to arrive in his absence, from his employer and from his wife; and Mrs Turnbull has returned them to me (enclosed).'" Robin reached out to the parcel on the table and unwrapped the heavy paper. The stack of my unopened letters fanned upon the table-top. (It is cliché to write my heart was in my throat, but it truly was—I felt that I could, indeed, choke to death at the spectacle.)

There was a final bit to the assistant constable's report which Robin hesitated to read, but elected to go forward with after a minute or two (I sat in silent and stunned disbelief, staring now at the returned letters, two dozen or more, unopened, unread, in fact *untouched* by your hand). "'The coast is approximately three miles from Mrs Turnbull's boardinghouse. To be thorough, I continued my enquiry at the port village of Tay, where I learned that several men matching the general description of Mr Saville have been seen in recent weeks. Not all of them could be he, or maybe none were. I further learned of two drowned men washing upon strands, some miles distant and days apart. In both cases the men had been in the sea for days, perhaps weeks, and were unidentifiable. One was believed

to be a local fisherman who was lost during a storm.
That fisherman's family claimed the body even though
the poor soul was unrecognizable. They may have
known nothing of the other drowned man, whose un-
claimed remains were interred unmarked by authorities in St Mark cemetery, in the corner reserved for
the poor and destitute. Moreover, at times the owners
of small fishing vessels will ferry passengers for a fee. I
located two who ferried men approximating Mr Saville's description during the period of interest. Neither
passenger called himself Philip Saville. One fellow was
taken north, to Aberdeen; the other south to Whit-
by. In a word, my enquiries were *inconclusive*. Some
of the information I gleaned is provocative, but nothing more. I was able to ascertain neither the fate nor
whereabouts of Mr Saville. Yours in Due Diligence,
Seymour Grey, County Angus Assistant Constable.'"

Even in my utter despair I wonder at the comic irony of Mr Grey's name—it is as ludicrous as the situation as a whole—and I wonder further if he cannot
see it himself, thus compounding the misplaced com-
edy. I hold in my trembling hand Mr Grey's pointedly
thorough report and copy it word for word, for that is
all I can do. Mr Pf has magnanimously forwarded to
Mr Peacock two months' salary for our keeping. Beyond that, it seems we are quite on our own in the
world. I have not told the children that their father
is . . . is what? That he is simply *gone*—the victim of
foul play, or of foul fate, or that he has removed himself elsewhere without a word. I continue to muse that

it is an elaborate and overplayed prank, and that at
any moment you will walk through the front door. I
even pause now, to listen, to hope, (I cannot prevent
myself) to pray—but there is nothing. The children
have not been informed, but they are not dullards—
far from it—so they sense something is terribly amiss.
They must be told soon, yet I find it more appealing
to sit here *writing* that I must break the news to them
rather than actually breaking it. I think continually of
receiving word that my father had died when I was a
girl, and I recall with clarity the shock and the pain of
it, the pure terror. I remember feeling that I had been
enveloped in the blackest of bunting, which appeared
to creep everywhere in our mourning, like a ferocious
fungus, and I should never see the light of day again.
How can I be the mechanism of their pain and misery,
the facilitator of their suffocating fear?

I again pause to listen.

nothing

Sept 24 (or is it the 25th?).

Dearest Philip,

Perhaps I continue to write to you, with no intention of posting the letter but merely to add it to this
collection of unopened correspondence, because it
helps me to believe you are still in this world, called
away for reasons I cannot fathom but making your way
back to us; and so one day soon you will read all the
words I have committed to you—to your eye, to your
ear, to your head, your heart. Perhaps writing to you

is simple habit. I have written with such consistency I cannot now just stop. I would be like the opium fiend who tried to cut himself off from the fruit of the poppy of a sudden; I too would be a desperate case, more desperate than I already am. Perhaps I write because if I were to *not* it would be the first act of letting go of you, and I cannot do that. Again, I would be a desperate case, shattered into a thousand scattered pieces. Of good to no one.

Yesterday I spoke to Felix and Agatha. I did not tell them everything—every detail of Mr Grey's report—and I may have left them with more hope than I should; but I enacted the most brutality upon them of which I was capable. Mercifully they are somewhat distracted by the dog—the one who did me a good turn in the alley that day. She (yes, he is actually a *she*) managed to follow me home and appeared in our own alley. I did not relate the stray's history to the children, thus it may have surprised them that I was amenable to keeping her. Felix has named her Peachum, or Peach. Peach slept last night in the washroom. Mrs O will prepare a bath which she assures me will rid Peach of her fleas and other such vermin of the street. She has departed on a mission this morning to procure the bath's necessary ingredients.

I spoke to Mrs O about you with somewhat more candor than I did the children. She said nothing, but surprised me with a maternal embrace of comfort.

Robin has also departed on this somberly beclouded morning as he has an appointment with Mr Pea-

cock, no doubt regarding our finances. He received
the note from Mr Peacock requesting the visit in last
evening's post. I would have perhaps been the more
natural choice to summon to him, as I have been
managing the household expenditures these many
months, whereas Robin possesses only the scantest
notion of what they may be; but it seems Mr Pf and
Mr P now consider Robin the man of the house, so
therefore, due to the fact of his masculinity, he is better suited to consider the practical matters of money.
Or it may be that they conjecture I am in no state of
mind at present to think rationally—and in this they
may be correct. Reading back over what I have scrib-
bled, the sentences suggest more lucidity than I myself am sensing. In reality my mind is a snarled net of
contradictory thoughts and competing images, each
mental picture, no matter how illogical, fighting for
fleeting dominance:

You went for a walk in the woods (remember your
enthusiasm for hunting mushrooms?) and injured
yourself or fell ill miles from help. You returned from
a business call and were fallen upon by robbers who
believed your pockets were fat with currency. You
hiked to Tay to try your luck at fishing and ended
somehow among the waves and were carried out to
sea by a treacherous tide. You borrowed an unruly
mount to call on more distant clients and suffered a
fall, striking your head and dashing your memory,
thus you wander unable to tell even good Samaritans
your name or how to find your family. Any day your

recollections shall return, and you shall return to us.
You had a taste for jam and knew where there were
jars in your landlady's cellar, so you ventured down,
perhaps in the near dark, lost your footing, and you,
with your broken ankle, have been living on preserved
fruit all this while. You heard of potential markets to
expand the firm's business and took the initiative to
make some exploratory enquiries, keeping Mr Pf in
the dark should your efforts prove fruitless. You met
a woman who does not constantly remind you of the
death of Maurice. Or, you felt the tug of independence, sensed the carefree lightness of the bachelor's
freedom. You have found other lodging, perhaps even
more temporary than Mrs T's boardinghouse, so have
not bothered to inform anyone of your change of address. You have been kidnapped and held for ransom,
but the inept kidnappers are unable to communicate
the demand. You felt the urge to mushroom hunt but,
out of practice, you procured the wrong variety and
are poisoned, thus suffering fantastic visions which
prevent you from exiting the woods. You have been
contacted by a solicitor in regards to a possible inheritance and have journeyed to a distant place to press
your claim, only to become entangled by the courts.
Mrs Turnbull has murdered you and has, in fact, sold
all of your belongings.

　　You were wanting some sea air so traveled to Tay,
where a fisherman offered to take you out, but a sudden
storm blew the boat miles upon the ocean, and now
the bark's hapless captain is making his way home. Mr

Grey found you quite hale but is keeping the knowledge from us for his own designs. The business opportunities in Dundee are so plentiful you have decided to establish your own firm, in direct competition with Pfender & Sons, and are engaged in laying the foundation in utmost secrecy. Mr Pfender placed you in harm's way for his own profit and knows precisely what has become of you. You went for a stroll when you encountered an elderly neighbour struggling with his garden, thus you offered to help but in the process sliced yourself with a muddy trowel and are battling a raging fever, weakened and delirious. You inexplicably elected to execute Mr Franklin's kite experiment and were struck by lightning. Again in the woods, you cross paths with a trio of wolves. Again in the woods, you encounter the Hairy Man of Mr Smythe's traveler's tale. Again in the woods, you meet a troll from beneath a bridge you are attempting to traverse.

Or at sea, your small boat is beaten to smithereens by a whale bent on its destruction. You have been swallowed by said whale and shall one day be belched upon a beach somewhere. Or at sea, it is not a whale but a creature from the deep, a leviathan in the throes of bloodlust, an ancient seaman's myth made real. A gigantic squid who squeezes the boat until it bursts into an explosion of splintering boards. A shark the size of a ship.

My mind will not cease its furious spinning of fantastic and fatalistic tales. Worse than falling prey to accidents, to beasts, and to cruel circumstance are

the scenes of an entirely different sort of horror. You,
returned to your ancestral home, stroll through the
city's market stalls with your new love, mysterious behind her fan of black lace, in shadow avoiding the brutal midday sun. There are laughing children trailing
behind you, yours, vibrant and vivacious, resembling
their mother, with her thick ebon locks and hypnotic brown eyes. The dark rings of wood in my writing
table transform into the eyes of the new Mrs Saville,
Señora Saville. Her smoldering orbs stare at me mock-
ingly. I am sickened by my fancy, which will not re-
lent even for a blessed moment. I stop recording their
thick-comings only because my hand cramps into a
claw, my entire arm aches, throbbing in rhythm to the
hurt in my head. And my heart.

Days have passed; I cannot say how many. We
have entered the tenth month. There is little point in
attempting to record in any detail the elapsed time,
most of which remains shrouded in fog, which may
be just as well. Robin, in an effort to calm me, for-
bade me to write. However, the rest that he enforced
upon me had the opposite outcome. My agitation, apparently, became greatly heightened. Dr Higgins was
summoned. He administered a draught of some sort,
no doubt an opiate mixture of his own design, and I
slept—if 'sleep' one may call it. Days and nights, often
indistinguishable, of ceaseless dreaming, a perpetual
carnival of disturbing visions and terrible imaginings
which presented themselves as quite real. Perhaps they

were, and this is the nightmare. In addition to Robin and Mrs O'Hair and the children, I recall a stream of visitors to my bedside: The doctor of course, and Mrs Shelley, Rev Grayling, even the kindhearted Mr Smythe; but also you, Philip (at times with your new wife and family), Maurice, who spoke words of comfort and lay beside me, an older version of himself, and the cutthroat in vivid green, as menacing as ever; Mr Havens, the Geographic Society undersecretary, looked in on me as well—it must have been an opiate-induced hallucination, as were the livestock that stood staring at me here and there in the bedroom, cows at times, swine and sheep at others. Or it was their butchered remains which lay scattered across the floor. In the nights especially I woke to a dark presence in the room, disquieting in its silence, disturbing in its stillness. I searched for it in the dark but found only its greater darkness. In some ways this haunting figure felt more corporeal than the gauzy ghosts of the living who paid me visits like watchers at a wake.

During my stretch of insensibility Robin hatched a plan, one that is perhaps *desperate*, but that word describes precisely where we find ourselves. Looking back through these pages of erratic prose, I find that I have not described our situation, as it was illuminated to Robin upon his visit to Mr Peacock. I thought I had written about the meeting. It is no wonder I am befuddled. Robin's report after returning from Mr Peacock's is what sent me over the edge, as it were—the dromedary's proverbial backbreaking straw. I hesitate to put it into words for fear it may undo me again. Yet I know I must come to terms with it, that denial of the truth shall not render it untrue. It seems, according to our banker, we are on the brink of destitution. He claims that you withdrew your set-aside money (your rainy-day fund) some time ago, nearly six months. It was a considerable sum after all these years of pinching every haypenny, just beyond £4,000 Robin was informed, thus we have been subsisting month to month on your salary from Pfender & Sons, which is soon to come to an end. What is more, Robin discovered that the house is heavily mortgaged. We will be lucky if the sale price balances the debt. I want to believe it is all a colossal error, a monumental mistake of accounting, but one which only you can correct, and, alas!, you are not here; nor, it seems, anywhere.

Adding to the ignominy, I learned that Mrs O'Hair has had a clearer sense of our dire situation than I and has been assisting in secret with household expenses out of her already modest salary. She reluctantly confessed the fact to Robin, who was struggling to make sense of the finances after I had fallen into the abyss. I can barely look Mrs O in the eye, so great is my shame. This was the situation in which my poor brother found himself: an abandoned sister, drugged to suppress her hysteria, a niece and nephew to support, an altruistic but aging housekeeper . . . and the wrecked remains of finances which are not even his own. In desperation he turned to his one friend, Mr Andropov, and together they devised a plan, and a radical one it is. I believe Robin was reluctant to provide me the particulars for fear it would result in my relapsing into the phantom-filled void from which I have only recently emerged. Yet at some point he must, so he did.

He and his mate are optimistic there is at least one more voyage remaining in the storm-tossed timbers of the *B Franklin*, thus they propose to sail her to America, at which point the plan must rely largely on improvisation. We shall sell the house and essentially all of its contents—every stick of furniture, every pot and every pan, nearly every book—to settle our debts and finance the one-way expedition, which Robin intends to make with a skeleton crew, whom Mr A has been busy procuring. He has also taken out notice for passengers and cargo whose transport will assist further with expenses. Our destination is New York City and then the heavily wooded Hudson Valley, where Mr A believes he may be able to put his carpentry skills to greatest advantage. Once arrived, Robin shall sell the *Franklin* to provide our keeping until other means are secured.

In spite of the turmoil of the last few weeks he completed his paper for the Geographic Society and has made a chapter outline for a book-length work. Mr Havens has arranged for Robin to give a brief talk to the Society, undoubtedly his last official act as captain of the *Franklin* on English soil. Meanwhile, Mr H has reached out to kindred societies in New York, Boston, and Philadelphia on my brother's behalf; moreover, he shall act as agent to find an English as well as an

American publisher for Robin's book once it is written. It seems my brother has warmed to the funny little fellow, and has placed great trust in him. Mrs O'Hair is not inclined to make the journey. Mr Smythe will take her on for some light duties. In yet another astonishing turn, she and the coalmonger's man, Bob, are planning to wed and set up house nearby. The resourceful Mrs O located remnants of oddly cut bolts of heavier fabric, and is making sufficient clothing for our crossing and then wintering in America. Most of the pieces are patchwork creations which are far from fashionable but greatly appreciated—even absent, the Irishwoman will help to ensure our survival.

I read back over my words, and Robin's mad plan has a matter-of-course tone which belie these extraordinary developments. I claim as excuse for the inadequacy of my pen that I am still in shock and see everything somewhat at a distance, as one may view the strange unfoldings of a theatrical plot. None of it feels quite real. I was puzzled as to why we could not sell everything, including the ship, and simply start again here, but Robin is adamant that we must leave England. For reasons he is unable to make clear to me, we must get as far away as possible. His resolve would suggest our very lives may depend on it. Having to take control of the situation and orchestrate our speedy exodus has been precisely what Robin needed to regain his health and vigor. He was languishing in the role of houseguest and needed, apparently, to return to the forecastle of his own ship to feel himself again.

I, on the other hand, do not wish to do any of it, my dear. I wish for you to walk through the front door and explain this amazing misunderstanding. I wish for us to laugh about it all. I wish for us to resume our life here on Corum Street, in this house, which in a matter of days shall no longer be ours. Yet I am also thankful for Robin, whose return was the very emblem of fortuitousness, of serendipity. I do not know how I would have coped by myself with these vicissitudes. I suppose, out of necessity, I would have, but how remains a mystery I hope never to solve.

Nov 5ᵗʰ. I am sorry, my darling, I have not written for days. Attending to the never-ending list of details has required all of my attention and nearly all my energy. We have been under pressure to finalise arrangements for our departure as Robin fears further delay and the increased likelihood of winter storms on the Atlantic. It is nearly too late to attempt the crossing already. Amidst all the hubbub Robin completed his paper and presented it before the Geographic Society in a specially organized meeting, arranged by the dogged Mr Havens. It seemed to be well received. The hall of course does not admit women, but Mr H obtained permission for me to listen to the presentation from a side corridor by which the cooks and maids come and go as they provide service to the Society's esteemed members.

Felix and Agatha, meanwhile, appear excited for the adventure; preparations have been a useful distraction. I continue to plan for our departure in spite of my inability to accept your utter vanishing; and I still hold out a sliver of hope you shall return to us. As such, I am entrusting Mr Smythe with the letters, the ones I wrote to you which were returned unopened, those straggling few marked 'Return To Sender' in what must be Mrs Turnbull's forceful script, and these most recent additions. The hope is that you will come looking for us and will enquire of Mr S what has become of your family. Once we have established a place for ourselves with some permanence I shall send to Mr S the details—so that you can follow us to America.

I cannot think of a better stratagem for our reunion. I want you to know, Philip, my dearest, that no matter what has happened to separate us—even if you feel somehow you are at fault—it does not matter: I can forgive you anything, if necessary. I grew up fatherless and shall do whatever I must to save the children from my fate, especially Aggie, for I do believe that little girls need their fathers more than little boys need their mothers. I cannot say on what this belief is based other than on my own fractured childhood. So, please, *please*, my dear, if you are still part of this world, find us, find your wife and your children—no matter where we land in the foreign fields of America.

Nov 6th. I woke in the night in terror, drenched in my own perspiration. I sensed the dark presence again, but this time I was able to identify it, to identify *him*. The presence was Maurice; however, not our little dove as some malevolent ghost, but rather a heartbroken wraith, for we must leave him behind. I am ashamed to admit I had not thought of that, amid all the frantic arranging of things. We must leave our little boy here, lying in a lonely, unvisited grave, while we seek a new life thousands of miles across the ocean. How can I leave him? The first separation nearly killed me; surely this one shall finish the task. I thought I heard him weeping in the dark. I lit my candle so that I could find him and comfort him. In the sudden glow of the candlelight I was startled to see him so plainly. I called him to me and embraced him. I held our child, returned from the grave, for a long while before he spoke and I realised it was not Maurice in my arms but rather Felix, who had woke to his own nightmare, though he could not recall what it was about—only the palpable terror it had shed like a skin. I understood then there was no help for leaving behind Maurice; my only choice was to choose a new life for my living children. There, in the candle's weak light, I had the thought that if you are not among the living, perhaps you have found your little boy in the night world of death—you can embrace him *there*, as I embrace our children *here*. Together we can comfort and console all three. The odd idea eased my pain.

These reflections have reminded me of Mrs Shelley, who has had her own strange turn of events during my visitation to the abyss. Her stepsister, a Miss Imlée, with whom she had been close, took her own life. Mae was not forthcoming as to how or why, and I felt it would have been ghoulish of me to press for details.

One positive from the sad affair was that it brought Mr Shelley out of hiding, and he and Mae are reunited under a single roof. That is not all. I hesitate to record anything further for fear of appearing a common gossip-monger—but can one be a gossip when writing details in a letter which likely will never be read? All this time my reference to Mae as 'Mrs Shelley' has been premature. The couple has only recently been married. Prior to this union under the auspices of the law, their bond as man and wife had been strictly spiritual. They had been mated in their souls since their very first meeting, Mae told me. It seems the existence of a lawful Mrs Shelley—Percy's *first* wife—had been standing in the way of their legal union; however, the unexpected passing of that Mrs Shelley, via circumstances which are unclear to me, made way for Mary to take up the mantle officially. Mae has been a regular visitor since my return from the terrible chasm. In fact, I believe it was she who convinced Robin that his preventing me from writing, no matter how well-intentioned, was counter-therapeutic. Mrs Shelley, meanwhile, continues to struggle with the book she is attempting to pen. The dramatic twists and turns of her real-life narrative have provided continuous distractions and interruptions, which, I sense, are frustrating on the one hand, but also a welcome relief from the pressure she feels to write something publishable that may bring some modest pecuniary assistance to her growing family. I sympathise fully.

Nov 11th. Our voices echo eerily in the house for it

is practically empty. Mr Squire carted away the last of the books two days ago, except for the volumes we are keeping (mainly to mollify Felix's bibliophilia), which have already been packed onto the *Franklin*. She is scheduled to set sail on the morrow. Mr Peacock has seen to the sale of the furniture and other household items—all has been either liquidated or sent to storage until buyers' offers can be confirmed. It seems he may purchase the house himself, or his company. I am not clear on the details as Robin has seen to the specific arrangements. I am certain he would share them with me, but in truth I am, well, disinterested. I find that my mind alternates between considerations of the uncertain future and recollections of the dim-becoming past, which already feels like a series of distant memories, or even someone else's history altogether. A life I read in a book. Meanwhile, the here-and-now has been a long list of tasks which must be accomplished; and after weeks of diligent attention, that list is nearly completed.

Since the house is all but empty, Mr Smythe kindly offered that the children and I spend our final evening in his rooms, where he would be delighted to make up some 'sleeping quarters', as the old military officer phrased it. We declined, preferring to spend the night here, with blankets on the floor of the parlour. Robin and Mr A have been staying aboard the *Franklin* for the last several days overseeing her final preparations. In the morning a carriage will transport the children and me from our old life to our new—I doubt much sleep shall be had by anyone. Without even a chair at my disposal, I write while seated on the floor, a book on my knees serving as small but serviceable desk-top (rather unladylike, I must confess). Before departing I shall add this final letter to the collection which Mr Smythe already has in his keeping, kept for you, or for no one.

I come to a point where I may be writing my final words to you, my love. It is not melodrama to call our crossing the ocean perilous. I hold out hope, even now, that I shall see you again, that the children shall see their father again. But I must acknowledge that that hope is a shrinking ember whose heat is nearly spent. Thank you, my darling, for the life you have given me, even with its episodes of sadness and this shocking conclusion. There also has been much joy and tenderness, much love and laughter—I will do my best to remember those moments most of all. I can think of nothing more to say. Imagine, I, finally out of words. Good night and good-bye, my dearest.

M

I feel compelled to add a brief postscript. When we rose this morning and Felix let Peach out into the alley, he discovered someone had left a parcel at our door. Felix brought it to me in the parlour, where I was organizing the last of our things and preparing to say farewell to Mr Smythe. The parcel was battered and stained, the address barely legible, which perhaps accounts for its long delay—yet it is a miracle it came through at all. I knew it immediately: the manuscript which Robin wrote while marooned on the ice, the Swiss scientist's tortured tale. I was befuddled as to what to do with the woebegone package. Robin obviously does not want it. I am curious, but there is no time to examine its contents—the carriage shall arrive at any moment. Maybe Mrs Shelley could find the papers useful. After all, she has been writing her tale of the Polar explorer. No doubt there are a plethora of details within which could aid the composition of her narrative. I shall leave the package with Mr S with instructions to forward it to Mae at his earliest convenience. Perhaps one day we shall read something by the young authoress and see reflected in it tiny shards of Robin's own tale, altered and arranged according to her authorial design, and it will be as close as I will ever come to knowing the terror my brother faced trapped there, at the boundary between the known and the unknown—a place, I realise, I suddenly find myself.

Additional Material

A Wintering Place

THE NOMADS OF THE STEPPES call me a name which loosely translates to 'Black Giant.' *Giant* is understandable, but the other. . . . Perhaps it is because of my hair, which has grown long down my back. I keep it tied with a leather thong. Perhaps it is because of my cloak—once a dark, rich leather which has been continually exposed to the elements and soaked in seawater several times. Then again, perhaps the nomads have the ability to see into my heart, for it too must be as black as midnight, as black as a vulture's wing, as black as the earth where my victims lie—their bodies strewn across three continents: Europe, Asia, and finally the Arctic. A zigzag trail of blood as crooked as the scars that cover my body like a taut snare. I have not killed—Man anyway—for a long time. Yet the blood seems fresh on my hands. The nomads must sense it too. They keep clear of me. When I have been spotted, they post triple the usual number of sentries for a few nights. No matter. I pass quietly through their encampment, a virtual city of tents, taking what I need. Only what I need—this is important—and only when I need it. Food usually, occasionally ammunition or matches. And I try to pay for what I take. Twice I left them bearskins, another time a leather pouch of herbs. Often I leave toys for their children— figures carved of wood or rock or bone. Animal shapes—bear, deer, squirrel, owl—and figures resembling their nomadic parents. Men with long mustaches and wide shoulders. Women with large eyes, full breasts and long straight hair. Once I carved a likeness of myself but I destroyed the hideous chunk of wood in the fire. I trust the elders give these trinkets to the children. I don't think they associate this covert form of barter with me. Surely they believe one such as I could not possibly slip into their camp, past their vigilant sentries, past their skittish blue-eyed dogs, past the wakeful mothers who fear for their babes. They fear sickness, they fear hunger, and they fear that the Black Giant will snatch them for his stew. Sometimes I hear them muttering about me in the night. I often linger in their camp, listening to their sounds, the walls of their felt tents doing little to insulate them from me. The whimperings of a feverish child, the gibberish of a delusional old man. Couples whispering long into the dark night about their hopes and troubles. Or sometimes I hear their lovemaking—such a foreign sound to my ears. Though I am in a sense a virgin, I somehow recollect the dance of it, and the smell and the taste of it. All of these things come flooding back to me—flooding back from the nameless void which is my past. There is no word, no phrase in any language for my origin. There was a married couple whose trouble was lovemaking. I would hear them fumble in their tent, then silence and sighing, then they would speak in voices below hearing. I could only detect the tone. The woman coos as if to an infant. His voice becomes increasingly agitated. Finally he walks in quiet fury from the tent and pisses in the dark. I see his steam rising in the light of a recently full moon. He is bare-chested in spite of the cold. I stay cloaked in shadow, as silent as a tree. The woman begins crying. I wanted to help them. I carved a phallus from ashwood. It took me days to shape and smooth the phallus. Often I was overcome with grief and loneliness and a painful sense of irony. Here I am, healthy and vital, full of love, and I have no one. When I was finished, feeling exhausted and empty, I crept into their tent city. I easily found the home of the troubled couple—I have the senses of a wolf—and I left the phallus outside their tent's opening. I wrapped it in a piece of my finest leather, so that they would know it was a gift and not a cruel joke. I have not been back to eavesdrop on their tent. I could not take another act of kindness being misunderstood and dismissed. It would plunge me into suicidal despair, yet I do not have the courage for suicide. I attempted it once, just after my father died. I stood at the northern rim of the world and set myself on fire. I writhed like a serpent. Then the ice must have cracked and I dropped into the frigid sea. I gulped in the salty water, trying to drown myself. I lost consciousness but awoke on a jagged raft of ice. Involuntarily resurrected once again. I recall little of the weeks that followed. Animal instinct for survival. I made my way south, back toward Man. Man, my cousin at least if not my brother. I have a sense that I made most of the journey on my hands and knees. I ate leaves and grass, much of which I vomited. I ate birds's eggs from their nests. The birds had no sense of how to defend their young against a predator such as I. At one point, my nadir, I found the droppings of a bear and chewed on the bits of undigested bone in its feces. Then one morning, before first light, I woke to the sound of human voices and the smell of horses. I thought I was hallucinating. It was a tribe of nomads en route to their wintering place. That night I had my first taste of bread in many months. I trailed them for days, and gradually, thanks to my thieving, my strength returned. One night I stole a rifle and a knife. The next day the nomads found a field-dressed buck in their path. They paused just long enough to prepare the venison for travel. The nomads finally reached their winter camp in a narrow valley between lavender mountains. I do not know the names of the peaks but they remind me of my father's beloved Mont Blanc. Living in the shadows of these mountains I have an odd feeling of reassurance. It was the day I decided to partially ascend one of the mountains that the nomads first saw me. I was on an exposed face of rock when a small hunting party spotted me. I heard their excited voices far below. Their word for *bear* drifted up to me but they must have quickly dismissed the notion. I was awkwardly making my way toward some cover when a bullet struck an outcropping of rock an arm's length away. It was a shot of experimentation, I am convinced: They wanted to see if I would react like Man or Beast. The nomads are expert marksmen. Even at that distance and odd angle, they could have shot me through the heart. I suspect their experiment proved inconclusive, and they had not a clue if I were Man or Beast. That night I heard the name 'Black Giant' for the first time. Already the tale had been elaborated. It seemed I was transporting the carcass of a bear cub up the mountain, and that when fired upon, I returned a volley of stones. Later I heard that I rolled a huge boulder down at them, narrowly missing their leader, whom I appeared to know instinctively. There was even talk that I was a winged creature and was in fact flying up the mountain. I have been more careful since, and they have only seen me at a great distance— which must exaggerate my size. To them I must truly appear eight feet tall, a height my father ascribed to me, but even though he was a man of science, a physician in fact, my father was prone to hyperbole. Unfortunately he was also prone to destruction, a trait I unfortunately inherited. Since my most recent resurrection, I have tried very hard not to succumb to that side of my nature. I have taken up lodging in an inconspicuous cave at the base of the southern mountain. I store my possessions here; I can cook my food in a small fire pit I have dug. To my astonishment I discovered a pool of fresh water in the back of the cave, where no light can penetrate. The water is so bracing it must be fed from high up on the mountain. I inspected the cave for a bear or puma or some other wild animal but there was none. Of course, bats reside in the cave, thousands of them. Their cacophonous squeaking just before dark was annoying at first. Otherwise they are tolerable fellow lodgers. This species of bat has enormous ears and no snout whatsoever, and it has a slightly sour taste, like that of rat. I was forced to eat rats when stowing away on a freighter bound for Arkhangelsk. The cats on the ship were more adept at catching rats than I, so I ate them too. I am not proud of the fare I have dined on. Man has forced this upon me as well. I am watching from near the entrance to my cave when a single rider approaches the tent city. He is dressed much like a nomad, including the coarse tunic and the knee-high felt boots, but his face is hairless. At first I think he is a boy. A small party from the camp rides out to meet him. They greet each other as friends but I note there is a subtle difference in their languages. Still, they invite him to proceed to their camp and the four horsemen ride in together. The event sparks my curiosity but I have to wait for darkness to fall. No matter. Probably all I will miss is the tending to the horses and an elaborate meal—not elaborate with food, but with formality and speeches. Man is so often preoccupied with ritual. There is a sliver of moon low in the eastern sky when I enter their camp. As I suspected, the stranger is in the tent of the elders, the political nucleus of the camp. I can hear the odd dialect of the stranger's voice amid the other voices in the tent. They are having a heated discussion in the language of the nomads. It involves family connections: 'Elka has been our responsibility for fourteen winters . . .' 'She cannot survive our way of life, it is not fair to the girl—' 'You speak of fairness, God cast that die fourteen years ago when He made her blind and crippled . . .' 'Surely someone among you—' 'There is no one, and Elka's parents unburden themselves, her father is not well, she is past the marrying age . . .' There is silence, then: 'Is she fertile?' 'Who can say? And if she is, no one wants to pass on the crookedness . . .' There is movement nearby in the dark. I realize my cheeks are wet—I fear I have been weeping aloud and will be discovered. It is not for my own safety I am concerned. I am afraid for theirs. My instinct for self-preservation is too strong for me to control. The sound is only young people sneaking around under cover of night—a boy and a girl going to steal kisses in the dark. I focus on the voices again: '. . . three days hence then, we will prepare for her arrival . . .' While returning to my cave I think about the woman-child. Snow is in the air and stings my wet face. I sit in the glow of my weak fire and imagine her deformities: 'blind' the stranger said, 'the crookedness' he said. Suddenly I am drowning in a maelstrom of bitter emotions—rage, despair, jealousy. . . . In my

mind's eye I see my own promised-one, carefully selected by my father. She is there, lying on his table,
completed. Then I watch her being butchered, the
rending of her lovely skin, the quick dismemberment,
the final—and superfluous—beheading. Death and
the female form. They are forever paired in my mind,
like freakish twins joined at the heart. I think too of
murdering my stepmother. There was more astonishment in her eyes—beautiful green eyes with flecks of
gold—than of terror as I strangled the life from her.
And there is the other female, the one who appears in
my dreams. A mere girl really. I can sense her anguish
and confusion. Also I can feel the impending doom
that covers her like a mourning gown. Death will be
her constant companion and she somehow knows it—
in spite of the opiate of youth. I do not recall the girl's
name. No, more than not recalling, I never knew it.
Yet I share an intimacy with her, a mother-child kind
of intimacy. Perhaps I am retrieving womb memories,
the interpretations of a fetus. But I have no recollections of boyhood, any boyhood. My fit in the cave
continues long into the night. At some point my fire
goes out but I do not care. Dark and cold are two of
my oldest friends. I wait for the arrival of Elka. I worry
that the snow that fell will delay her traveling; but it is
the fretting of an old woman. Only a finger's length of
snow is on the ground and it has already melted from
those places directly in the sun. On the third day,
about mid morning, four riders enter the valley of the
nomads. As they draw near I notice that one of the

riders is on a brown and white pony. This must be Elka. She is completely cloaked in a bearskin. Puffs of her breath come from the portion of the bearskin which forms a hood. Elka's pony is being led by the stranger who had visited the nomads originally. I want to see the blind girl's face but it is completely obscured. I once had a friend who was blind. It was as if a skin had grown over his eyes. I wondered if Elka's blindness was of the same type. I often thought that if I'd had a surgeon's skill—as my father did—I could have removed that second skin and given my friend the gift of sight. Yet it was his blindness which allowed him to befriend me. We never had the opportunity to pursue our friendship. Man drove us apart. Milton wrote of the Fallen Angel; I fell that day. Dare I wish for a companion? A female with whom to share the rest of my days? God appeared to decide otherwise some years ago. However, I have felt justified in questioning Him. It is a cold day. The sun is bright but it feels distant. Here and there, along the stream which feeds the valley, pools of water have formed a crust of ice. The stream flows less briskly. I stand in a grove of coniferous trees and watch the trickling water. In the days that I have waited for Elka a plan has formed in my mind. Truly, it seems to have taken shape of its own accord without any voluntary thought from me. So standing there among the trees, a cold breeze blowing my hair, I consider the plan as if it is being offered by some outside agent. In a few weeks spring will come to the valley, and the nomads will trek north, as their ancestors have done for generations. I will watch for the signs of it, and when they are on the verge of leaving I will take my Elka—yes, damn them all, she is mine!—and bring her to my cave. They will not delay their departure for long. Not to search for a poor blind girl they did not want in the first place. Then the nomads will leave the valley, and I will be alone with my Elka. Alone with my Elka: The idea of it makes me light-headed with joy. This is surely what is meant to be. Why else would my miserable life continue to be preserved? Who better to be the benefactor of the poor, the malformed, the wretched? So I wait. Nightly I creep into the camp, hoping to recognize her odd dialect coming from a tent, hoping to catch a glimpse of her by firelight. But again and again, I cannot find her. Is this a joke? Did I not see her ride into their camp? Was it a hallucination? Has this entire episode with the nomads been a hallucination? Perhaps I lie dying on an ice flow in the Arctic Sea, and in a few tortured hours I have imagined months of encounters with the people of the Steppes. No, it must be real. My love for Elka is real, my desire for her too. I must be patient. I must continue to stockpile provisions in my cave, so that when I bring my Elka home I will not have to leave her in search of food—not for many days. I do not like the thought of leaving her alone in the dark of the cave—though I know its blackness is insignificant compared to the blackness she has always known. Slowly spring has come. It rains almost daily. Buds are appearing on the earliest trees and bushes. Activity at the camp has changed; the nomads are preparing to leave. At last the day has come for them to tear down their tent city. I creep as close as I dare in daylight and watch as they pack their camp. Tonight they will sleep under the stars and at sun-up they will begin their long journey north. I must find where Elka will lie. There are so many men, women and children moving about. It is bedlam. I search frantically for her. Tears of frustration blur my vision. Finally I see a figure who is not running about. She is seated by a fire, the bearskin around her shoulders. Some final tents were blocking my view of her until they were taken down. I strain to see her eyes, her nose, her mouth but Elka's hair is hanging down. Here we are, on the eve of our union, and I still do not know my lover's face. My heart is racing. I notice that a thunderstorm appears to be building in the north. If it does not delay the nomads' departure, the storm could work to my benefit. I do not move. The day wanes. The nomads prepare their meals. They tend to their animals. Then they sleep next to their fires, which smolder more than burn. It must be approaching midnight when the first drops of rain fall. They are heavy and cold. The wind has come up and thunder follows lightning at a close distance. The streaks of lightning seem to be tinted red—perhaps a trick of the mountains. I should probably wait for the storm to pass but I cannot. My patience has been exhausted. I move from my hiding place; my limbs are stiff at first. I stay low to the ground—as low as a being of my stature is able. A flash of lightning momentarily brings daytime to the valley. I must be careful. My feet, wrapped in strips of leather, slip in the mud and I nearly lose my balance. I must make certain to take a circuitous route back to the cave for my footprints will be easy to track in the mud. The nomads have posted some sentries but they are huddled under tarpaulins smoking their pipes. I reach their camp and crawl on my hands and knees between packed bundles and smoldering fires. When lightning streaks across the sky, I freeze and try to resemble just another bundle. The thunder is a cannonade. I reach the group of bodies where Elka is sleeping; I can smell the musk of the wet bearskin she is wrapped in. Lightning flashes and I see her long tousled hair. I am an arm's length from my Elka! Short of breath, I reach out and gently touch her hair. Even wet, her hair feels like silk, which I have only touched once before: The gown my stepmother was wearing when I murdered her was of silk. The instant the next bolt of lightning has receded I snatch up my Elka. She weighs nothing. I carry her, bearskin and all, as a mother carries her newborn, except I keep my hand over her mouth, careful not to also cover her nose. I am touching my Elka's face! I want to see her but it is too dark and I am moving too quickly. I must keep my balance. I can feel her deformities through the animal skin. Her back is hunched. Her legs are as thin as broomsticks and they are not connected quite right to her pelvis. Elka is perfect. She is trying to scream but my hand prevents it. We are some distance from the camp when a ruddy lightning flash illuminates the valley and I hear the shouts: 'The Black Giant!' 'He's got hold of something!' I quicken my pace as best I can in the mud. At a great distance or just muffled in the rain, I hear: 'Elka—the Black Giant has Elka!' Their dogs began to bark and bay. God, what are you doing to me now? I try to run but my foot slips and I go down on one knee. I recover and continue. Elka is thrashing about in terror. I want to get her to my cave—all will be well there—but I know my path must be serpentine. I sense that the no-mads are following me. I did not expect this reaction. After all, Elka was unwanted by both her clans. I know where there is a depression in a grove of trees. Perhaps I can hide there until they stop searching, which will surely be soon. I make my way there, slip down the hill, and carefully lay Elka on the ground. I cover her with my arms, keeping my hand over her mouth. The trees shield us from the lightning flashes. So with the dark and my hand and the wet hair matted to her fore-head, I still do not know my lover's face. She is horri-fied. I try to calm her—'It is all right, I will not harm you'—but I find I have not mastered the nomads's lan-guage, particularly her clan's dialect. My words must sound like the gibberish of a lunatic. The violent part of the storm has abated somewhat but it is still raining hard. The drops are loud in the tree limbs. Mist hangs in the air like vengeful spirits. Elka's heart beats furi-ously against my forearm. I can see torches through the trees and the nomads are calling her name. At first they are in front of me then the searchers seem to be all around. The rage of a trapped animal begins to swell in me. I realize that Elka is not struggling as she had been; perhaps she is exhausted. I whisper, 'Please, do not scream,' and cautiously take my hand from her mouth. She does not. Because I cannot see her still, I touch her face. Her eyes are deep set, her nose is strangely but gently curved as if molded of clay, her jaw is set irregularly and feels thicker on one side. She is perfect and I love her desperately. The searchers continue to call her name. Some of them are close. I struggle to keep my sobbing from giving me away. I pick her up again; this time she does not fight. I carry Elka up the slippery hill and place her in the open. I kiss her hair, then return to the grove of trees. I listen as she calls to her people. They quickly locate her and begin conveying her back to camp. I watch as the torchbearers come together. All I can see are their crimson flames. They appear to merge into a single blaze. When all is quiet I make my way to the cave. I look at the piles of provisions. Then the words of the poet come to me: 'As one who in his journey bates at noon, Though bent on speed; so here the Arch-Angel paused, Betwixt the world destroyed and the world restored. . . .' By the end of summer I must find somewhere else. I will go east or west. But I cannot be in the valley when the nomads return to their wintering place.

Afterword

IT MUST HAVE BEEN 1986 that I first read Mary Shelley's *Frankenstein*. I was taking a correspondence course (the forerunner of the online course) from the University of Iowa in the History of Science Fiction (or maybe the Evolution of Science Fiction, something like that), and a box filled with books arrived from the university's bookstore. The first title on the syllabus was *Frankenstein*. It must've been then that I learned Mary Shelley's book was considered by most the first science fiction novel. In creating her monster, she had created a whole genre. I don't recollect loving the book. In fact, I remember its being a bit of an uphill climb (I am loathe to admit). I suppose like just about all first-time readers, the novel surprised me; it wasn't what I'd been conditioned to expect by a culture which had transformed Mary Shelley's story into a tale about a mad scientist who creates a horrid monster that runs amok through the countryside. In reality, the monster spoke, eloquently even. He was philosophical, introspective. He inspired sympathy.

I also wasn't prepared for Mary Shelley's florid prose. Back then, I was still in my Vonnegut phase. I loved short, pithy sentences laced with humor, especially gallows humor. Mary Shelley's sentences were none of those things. I also had an infant son who was mainly my responsibility. I have no complaints about that, but wading through Shelley's novel in between bottles and diapers and strolls and baths wasn't the ideal way to absorb *Frankenstein* and notice all that its young author was up to. I was a neophyte schoolteacher who had thoughts of becoming a university professor or a full-time writer: considerations which may have also impeded my ability to read the book for what it was.

Time passed. I stayed in the profession, earning my M.A. along the way and adding two more sons to the brood, and in 1998 I got the opportunity to teach the sorts of things I'd always wanted to teach: Advanced Placement Literature and Senior English (meaning British Lit). I was able to design my own curriculum, and one of the first titles I selected was *Frankenstein*. In the intervening years I'd known teachers who swore by the novel, plus Kenneth Branagh's movie version had come out in 1994 and claimed a lot of ink. The book has remained on my reading list for twenty years (and the film is an annual favorite as well).

I had no inkling while I soldiered through that first reading how influential *Frankenstein* would be in my life, not only my teaching life but also my writing life. That florid prose style that seemed so foreign in 1985 completely captivated me when I returned to the text in 1998. I loved reading the novel aloud to my students. But even more so, I loved discussing the things the book is about. The issues it broaches and the questions it raises seem timeless: What are the potential risks and rewards of manipulating nature? What are our responsibilities to our creations? How human must something be to be afforded human rights? Is evil innate, or must it always be manufactured? These questions and countless others.

The language, the characters, the setting, the tone, the ideas all carved themselves into my cranium, fertilized my frontal lobe, burrowed into my brain, as I encountered the book year after year. I returned to it as reliably as salmon do their native streams.

Over time, Mary Shelley and her words would inspire in me a short story and two novels (at least). My first crack at writing based on *Frankenstein* was the short story "A Wintering Place" (reprinted in this volume). I don't recall when I wrote it, around 2000, give or take a year or two. At the time I wasn't putting a lot of effort into getting my work published, so it would be a number of years (2008?) before it was included in the journal *Eleven Eleven* (issue six). At the end of *Frankenstein*, the creature claims he's going to kill himself and our final image is his drifting away on a raft of ice; however, we don't witness his demise—a fact which paved the way for a plethora of sequels, including my story, in which I imagine that he attempted to commit suicide but was unable to overcome his innate will and ability to survive.

My story is set in an imagined version of Siberia. I felt it was my best writing to date. I enjoyed the fictive Siberian setting, and I also enjoyed working in a revisionist mode, composing a sequel to a novel I loved. The experience inspired me to try the approach again, this time, however, working on a sequel to Homer's *Odyssey*, another tale I loved and taught regularly. I decided to keep the Siberian setting. The story, though, wouldn't remain a story, and kept expanding into what would become my first published novel, *Men of Winter*.

In 2002 I began working on my Ph.D. in English studies at Illinois State University. The department didn't allow a creative-writing dissertation, so I embarked on several years of writing exclusively in an academic mode. It was difficult. On the one hand, I loved the courses and the scholarly writing I was pursuing, but on the other I missed writing fiction (ideas for stories and novels piled up in my brain like logs on the hearth, just waiting to be ignited). Nevertheless, I persevered, one course at a time, and eventually completed my doctorate in 2009.

My progress was steady, but in the summer of 2007 I found myself at a place where there wasn't much I could do toward my degree. I had one course remaining, the doctoral seminar in rhetorical theory, which would not be offered until the fall. After completing that course I could begin to prepare for my comprehensive exams (roughly a year's process), and after that came the writing of the dissertation (another year at least). I'd had an idea for a novel for a long while, inspired by the rumor of a romantic relationship between Mary Shelley (widowed after Percy's accidental drowning) and the American author Washington Irving (of "Sleepy Hollow" and "Rip Van Winkle" fame). I wondered what such a relationship would be like, true or not, what sorts of energy it could generate.

Even though I knew I could only begin writing the book before putting it aside to focus again on my doctoral work, that summer I started composing. I decided early on to not have the main characters be Mary Shelley and Washington Irving precisely, but rather to be inspired by their lives and personae (as we've come to think of them). I decided to write in the voice of my Irving-like character, whom I named Jefferson Wheelwright. The creative-writing part of my brain finally unbound, like long-suffering Prometheus, the prose poured from me, and by the beginning of August I had drafted sixty to seventy manuscript pages.

Then it was time to return to my doctoral pursuits. More than two years would go by—taking the final seminar, preparing for and passing my comps, writing and defending my dissertation—and throughout the process I kept thinking of Jefferson Wheelwright and my Mary Shelley character, Margaret Haeley, eager to return to their story. I successfully defended my dissertation in October 2009, and literally on the drive home that evening (about an hour's commute) I began planning the continuation of the narrative.

It would take a few more years of steady writing, but I completed the over 400-page manuscript in the voice of Jefferson Wheelwright (a voice one reviewer described as "a post-modernist emulating Henry James"), and went about trying to find a publisher. In the meantime, I'd begun my own small press, Twelve Winters, fashioning it after Leonard and Virginia Woolf's legendary Hogarth Press. The manuscript generated some interest, but ultimately there were no offers of publication, so I brought it out myself, in January of 2014, as *An Untimely Frost*. It garnered some good reviews but otherwise came and went leaving barely a ripple.

Sometime before then I got the idea for another Mary Shelley-inspired book. The entire epistolary novel of *Frankenstein* is addressed to Robert Walton's elder sister, Margaret Saville, about whom we know almost nothing, other than she lives in London and is worried about her brother on his polar expedition. That's it. Margaret Saville's name sits at the head of one of the most famous novels in the English language, yet she has remained a total mystery since its publication in 1818. There has been considerable scholarly attention paid to Margaret Saville, but to my knowledge no one had attempted to flesh her out, so to speak, via creative writing—to allow her to tell her own version of events in the world created by *Frankenstein*.

It would be awhile, however, before I would get

around to writing the book. Writing *An Untimely Frost* had been a very isolating experience, artistically speaking. I didn't send out portions of it for excerpted publication (in retrospect, I wish I had), so I went a long while without any editorial contact and, thus, validation. I decided for my next project I would write something that would allow me to circulate it and publish it in pieces in literary journals before bringing it out as a whole book. As I began I had a vague notion that I wanted it to be something like James Joyce's *Dubliners* or Sherwood Anderson's *Winesburg, Ohio*, an ambitiously experimental collection with reoccurring characters and the stories all set in the same location. I worked for four years on what would become *Crowsong for the Stricken*, like *Dubliners* and *Winesburg* but different from them, too.

I ended up calling *Crowsong* a "prismatic novel," but it wasn't quite the same as working on an honest-to-goodness novel, the writing of which was a process I was itching to return to. It was about two years between finishing *Crowsong* and bringing it out in book form. I had to wait for the last of the journals that had accepted parts of it to publish them, which happened in the summer of 2017, so *Crowsong for the Stricken* came out in August of that year. Meanwhile, I'd started working on *Mrs Saville* in 2015. I had the first two letters (chapters) written when I was sidetracked by my academic publisher's interest in releasing my doctoral dissertation as a book, which required me to revise and update my dissertation, and (yuck) write a detailed index. Much of the remainder of 2015 and the winter/spring of 2016 was devoted to that project. I'd also started, on a lark, to write what I thought would be a brief short story (a month's needed distraction from index writing—yuck).

Luckily, though, I'd sent out the first letter of *Mrs Saville* as a stand-alone piece, and in the summer of 2016 Jose Varghese, editor of *Lakeview Journal*, offered to bring it out in the fall. I'd long been fascinated by the process of writing and publishing via serialization, a practice which was quite popular in the nineteenth and twentieth centuries, when print magazines were in their heyday. How would writing for serial publication—as Dickens had, as Thackeray had, as Gaskell, Conan Doyle, Trollope and James had—affect one's process? I approached Jose with the idea of bringing out all of *Mrs Saville* via serial publication. He was interested but felt *Lakeview Journal* wouldn't be the ideal venue, since he only planned to publish two editions a year. But he also edited *Strands Lit Sphere*, an online extension of the journal, and he offered to publish the bits and pieces of *Mrs Saville* there as I wrote them.

At first, Jose's plan was to publish a chunk of the book every week. I broke up the first two letters into eight chunks, in other words, about two months' worth of serialization, and began work on the third letter in the fall of 2016. Around the holidays, otherwise known as the end of first semester in the academic world, Jose fell a bit behind, never quite to catch up again (let's be honest, no one was clamoring for the next installment of *Mrs Saville*, as readers had after *Oliver Twist* in Dickens's day). Ultimately, *Strands Lit Sphere* brought out about half the book, but Jose had provided much-appreciated support and motivation, and as a result I wrote *Mrs Saville* much faster than I had any of my previous books. I had a complete draft of the manuscript in hand by end of summer 2017, and I began the work of revising it (just as *Crowsong* came out in book form).

By the way, that "quick short story" I'd begun largely as a distraction from index writing (yuck) blossomed into my next novel, whose working title is "The Isolation of Conspiracy." As of this date, Parts I and II have been published here and there under various titles; an excerpt of Part III is forthcoming; and a handwritten draft of Part IV awaits further attention while I focus on composing Part V. I suspect there will be six parts all together. "The Isolation of Conspiracy" has no connection to Mary Shelley and *Frankenstein*, at least no obvious connection: I'm beginning to wonder if everything I write, if everything I've written, owes at least something to that gifted young woman and her weird, groundbreaking book.

Little did I know when I opened that big box arrived from Iowa City so many summers since.

Ted Morrissey
Sherman, Illinois
August 2018

About the Author

TED MORRISSEY is the author of two books of scholarship and seven books of fiction. His prismatic novel *Crowsong for the Stricken* won the International Book Award in Literary Fiction from Book Fest in 2018, as well as the American Fiction Award, and it was a *Kirkus Reviews* Best Indie Book of 2017. His novella *Weeping with an Ancient God* was a *Chicago Book Review* Best Book of 2015. His other books of fiction are *The Curvatures of Hurt*, *An Untimely Frost*, *Figures in Blue*, and *Men of Winter*. His short stories and novel excerpts have appeared in more than sixty journals, among them *Glimmer Train Stories*, *ink&coda*, and *Southern Humanities Review*. He holds a Ph.D. in English studies from Illinois State University. In addition to teaching high school English, he is also a lecturer in Lindenwood University's MFA in Writing program (online). He and his wife Melissa live near Springfield, Illinois. Together they have five children, one grandchild, and two rescue dogs. Ted founded Twelve Winters Press in 2012, modeling it after Leonard and Virginia Woolf's Hogarth Press.

Ted Morrissey's award-winning prismatic novel *Crowsong for the Stricken* is available in hardcover, paperback and Kindle editions.

Winner of the American Fiction Award in Literary Fiction
Winner of the International Book Award in Literary Fiction
(Book Fest 2018)
A *Kirkus Reviews* Best Indie Book of 2017

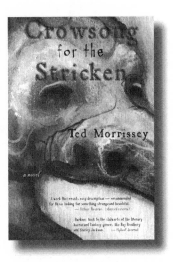

'A work that resists easy description —
recommended for those looking for something
strange and beautiful.'
— *Kirkus Reviews* (starred review)

'The language and the overall tone harken back
to stalwarts of the literary fantasy and horror
genres like Ray Bradbury and Shirley Jackson.'
— *Flyleaf Journal*

The Curvatures of Hurt, a Crowsong Universe Story, is available as an audiobook featuring the vocal artistry of Jenny Bacon.

Purchase on Audible, Amazon and iTunes.

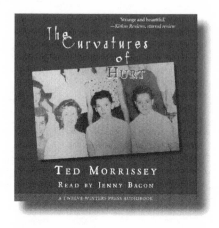

Also available in a companion paperback edition which includes an Afterword by Jenny Bacon.

Also by Ted Morrissey
from Twelve Winters Press

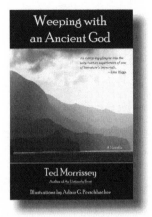

'An enticing read . . . It stands as a great little
work of existential crisis and isolation.'
— *Chicago Book Review*
A *CBR* Best Book of 2015

'A haunting journey through mid-19th-century
London . . . an engrossing mystery.'
— *North American Review*

Made in the USA
Columbia, SC
17 September 2018